She didn't want a close encou
wanted to avoid him if she pos........

"Aloha." His gaze went over her entire body. "The pleasure of meeting you is all mine Renée Colby." Her body began to tingle as he then lifted her hand to his mouth and gently kissed it. She suddenly felt an electrifying current rush through her body and she began to grit her teeth.

She thought to herself, "So this is Ja'Ron Moss." She didn't like the vibes that she was feeling from him. He was definitely breath taking, but she needed to remain focused. She didn't want this to be happening. Robert had done a number on her and she had to protect herself from being hurt by anyone else ever again.

His gaze traveled from her eyes down to her throat as he watched the lump form in her throat. "Something I've wanted to do since the first time I saw you." Without another word he swept her into his arms and kissed her. It was a nice, slow and seductive kiss. She wanted to stop him but couldn't find the strength too. *He's a great kisser.* He stopped and looked at her while he traced her cheekbones with his fingertips. "I have never been so drawn to any other woman before."

Hearing his last comment caused her mood to suddenly change and she frowned. She remembered when Robert spoke that same line with her and she had foolishly fallen for it. "Humph... Who do you think you're fooling?"

Aloha… A New Beginning

CHEVETTA BURTON

This book is dedicated to my beautiful three children, my granddaughter, and the love of my life. Special thanks and acknowledgement goes out to all my family and friends who have supported me in all my endeavors.

ISBN-13: 9781441485793
ISBN-10: 1441485791

Aloha… A New Beginning

Copyright © 2009 Chevetta Burton

All rights reserved. Unauthorized use of this work is prohibited without written permission from the author. Any unauthorized use of this work or any of its contents, in whole or in part, shall be considered copyright infringement.

This is a work of fiction. Names, characters, places, and incidents are either the product of the author's imagination or are used fictitiously, and any resemblance to actual persons, living or dead, business establishments, events or locales is completely coincidental.

Dear Reader,

Writing Aloha… A New Beginning was both exciting and rewarding for me. In this story, Ja'Ron Moss is a man determined to get whatever he wants and his eyes are on Renee Colby. I wanted to share with you how a successful business owner Renee Colby was able to open up and move from her past hurts and give love a chance again. Ja'Ron finally breaks through that wall she shields but then their relationship takes a turn once a family secret is revealed.

I hope you enjoy reading this story and I look forward to bringing you more in the near future.

I would love hearing from you, so please feel free to email me at cburton38522@yahoo.com.

    Blessings to All,

    Chevetta Burton

ONE

Tap, tap, and tap. "Mmmm…" Renée loved the wonderful sound of rain. Listening to the raindrops beating on the house, Renée laid in her bed thinking about how loneliness has become a part of her life. She flicked on the television and did her usual channel surfing. She frowned, "As usual nothing's on. I'll just keep the TV on the E channel." She liked to watch the fashion shows whenever she got a chance to. Recollecting her thoughts, she really hadn't done anything exciting since her divorce, which was final a few years ago. Dating was not a priority to her. Instead she spent more time building and planning the expansion of her business. Since the opening of Renée's Bridal Boutique a few years ago, business has been prosperous. It was the first African-American bridal boutique in the area, not to mention with excellent customer service. In a few months, she would be opening an entertainment hall, which would be managed by herself and her best friend Tiffany.

It brought her great joy to be able to satisfy her customers. She drowned herself with work so that left little or no time to socialize. Now that her business dreams were unfolding with much success she could begin to relax a bit. She could use some sort of change. Today was the first Saturday she had taken off in a while so she intended to enjoy herself, even if it was gloomy outside.

Renée switched sides wondering, "What shall I do today?" She needed to make a deposit at the bank and then she could go grocery shopping. "That won't take too long to do at all. What then?" she asked herself. She had the entire day with nothing really planned to do. Maybe she would catch a movie and then go out to dinner. She could call Tiffany. "Nay." She decided against that, figuring Tiffany was probably spending the day with her husband Keith. Listening to the telephone ring, she decided to let the answering machine pick the call up.

"Renée, I know you're there, pick up the phone."

Laughing as she pushed the talk button, "Tiffany darling hello."

"Cut the crap Renée; what's up girl?"

"Not much Tiffany. What's going on with you?"

"Girl, I'm so excited! Keith and I have decided to have a little get together at our place in a couple of weeks since we haven't done any entertaining in a while."

"Oh yeah!" Tiffany never has just a little get together. It always turns into something big and glamorous. Not to mention a lot of fun. Although Renée hadn't attended any of her parties since the divorce she'd helped her to plan and prepare them. As her best friend, she knew very well what her style was. This was not going to be something small.

"Yeah Renée and…."

She nodded her head a couple of times and replied in a dull tone, "I know, you want me to help you get everything together right?"

"Not only that Renée, you are attending this party also. I will not accept no as an answer either. It's going to be a blast and so many - well never mind. Everyone is dressing in Hawaiian attire. I'll be right over so that we can shop for our hook up. And we need to pick out the invitations today and get them in the mail."

She raised an eyebrow, not expecting Tiffany to demand her attendance. "But I'm not…"

"You're a beautiful thirty-one year old and completely free of any illness that would prevent you from attending. All you do is work, work, and work. Your chilling out at home every weekend is over. Love ya sweetie, see ya soon." Click Tiffany quickly hung up. She pasted a winning smile on her face. "Yes, work it girl. It's time for Renée to have some fun."

Renée recalled the first day the two of them met. She had started school a few days later than the rest of the children because she was recovering from the chicken pox. Her mom walked her to Ms. Chay's classroom on her first day of school. Renée didn't cry but she resented the fact that she had to be there.

She wanted to stay home with her mom. After her mom greeted the teacher she kissed Renée and assured her that she would be okay.

Renée walked around the classroom and she noticed another little girl standing by the window who resembled her. They both had caramel colored skin, almond shaped brown eyes with thick eyebrows, and long pretty black hair. The only clear difference was that the other girl's face was a little rounder. The teacher instructed everyone to take his or her seats. Everyone knew where to go except her. She had no idea where she was suppose to sit, so she moved to a remote area. The teacher then came over to where she stood and showed her where she would be sitting. She was seated next to the little girl she had seen by the window earlier.

They both had worn two long pretty ponytails and a designer overall short set. Renée wore purple and Tiffany wore baby blue. "Hi, my name is Tiffany. I like your outfit." Renée looked at her for a moment before turning her head. "Hey, why are you turning your head? I washed my face this morning, so I know it's not dirty. I brushed my teeth this morning, so I know my breath doesn't stink. And my mom let me wear some of her perfume. You want to smell my wrist?"

Renée shook her head and said, "No." She sure does talk a lot, Renée thought to herself. The teacher instructed the students to settle down.

Tiffany whispered in Renée's ear as she pointed across the room. "You see that boy over there; he's been watching you since you came in. I think he likes you." She started giggling.

Renée smiled back at her. "Didn't your mom ever tell you it's rude to point at people?"

"She sure did. But she's not here so she'll never know, right? It's our secret. So, what's your name?"

"Renée."

"It's nice to meet you Renée. We are going to be friends forever okay." They both smiled. "Let's shake on it," Tiffany continued as she held out her little hand. The two pretty little girls shook hands and they have been inseparable ever since.

Renée watched the end of the fashion show that was on before stretching one final time and deciding to get on up and out of her cozy bed. Now, thanks to her best friend, she didn't have to worry about what to do today. Any plans that she had would have to be postponed until Monday.

She ran a hot bath filled with bubbles. She figured she had plenty of time to soak since Tiffany was slow about getting dressed herself. She meant well but her idea of *right now* usually meant at least two hours later. As Renée sat in her soothing hot bath she began to wonder if she even knew how to party anymore – it had been so long. Robert and her used to attend social events together, but that was all over now. He was a lawyer and being the center of attention was his style. Unlike him, she didn't require spotlight attention all of the time. Attending parties was important to him so she tagged along for support. She sighed. "Support, yeah right." She was certain that he was still doing the same thing with someone else. "Jerk! Enough of that Renée don't dwell on the past." After bathing, she stepped out of the tub, dried off, put on some lotion, and slipped into her robe hanging on the back of the bathroom door.

Searching through the closet for something comfortable to wear, she decided that a T- shirt and a pair of jeans would be fine. It wasn't everyday she could dress like this, so whenever the opportunity arose she gladly took advantage of it. As soon as she finished dressing the doorbell rang. "That can't be Tiffany," she muttered.

"Coming," she shouted. Looking through the peephole, she saw that it was Tiffany. She opened the door and Tiffany strutted right in with much energy.

"Girl, Keith and I are so excited that you decided to come to the party. It's about time you start mingling again."

Renée rolled her eyes and sighed. "Whatever Tiffany, did I have a choice? You wouldn't let me say no remember?"

"Renée, what kind of friend would I be if I allowed you to stay in this house forever without meeting new people?"

Renée knew what she really meant was meeting a new man. "Just so you understand Tiffany I'm not going to your party to meet anyone to complicate my life." Trying to sound convincing she proclaimed, "At this time I'm perfectly happy with my personal life." She didn't want her to know about how she had been feeling earlier before she called.

"Yeah right. Who do you think you're fooling Renée? It's me Tiffany. No one wants to spend the rest of his or her life alone. Not even you. That's why… never mind. I'm surprised you're not ready to go yet." She followed Renée upstairs. "I fooled your behind this time didn't I? You probably thought I would be a couple of hours, huh?"

As they both laughed, Renée slicked her hair back into a ponytail, and put on a little lipstick. Then she slipped on a pair of shoes. "Ok Tiffany, I'm ready to go."

"Cool. I'll drive. Too bad it's raining today, we could of let our hair flow with the wind."

Keith had just purchased Tiffany a brand new royal blue Jaguar so she was more than happy to drive. The car was sharp as heck and the white leather interior was absolutely gorgeous. Keith had put some nice rims on the wheels also. "Tiffany maybe I should drive. I don't want to get carjacked."

Waving her hand, "No one is going to carjack us so don't even start tripping. Anyways, you know that BMW you're driving is off the hook. Trust me if someone wants this car they can have it because no material thing is worth my precious life. Besides, Keith would just have to buy me a new one."

"And we both know that he would buy your spoiled ass another one too."

They both laughed. All jokes aside, "I'm so happy that you have such a wonderful husband. So, is there a baby in tow yet?"

"Nope, but we're having fun trying." She chuckled. "I know it's gonna happen though so I'm not pressed. What do you think of the theme Keith and I came up with?"

"I think its cool Tiffany."

"Hawaiian Night! I can't wait," Tiffany exclaimed excitingly.

She then turned to Renée and said, "I know exactly what we are going to wear."

Pointing her finger Renée shouted, "Keep your eyes on the road please!"

"We are going to be knockouts," she continued ignoring the keep your eyes on the road comment.

With a frown she said, "Oh boy. I hate when you get like that. I know I'm in trouble now."

She patted her leg. "Girl it's cool, everything will be all right. First let's check out the mall to see what's there."

"OK."

They arrived at the mall and of course they valet parked, Tiffany wouldn't have it any other way. "Park safely," she said passing her keys over to the valet attendant.

"Yes ma'am," the attendant replied.

After a few hours of searching, to Renée's surprise they couldn't find anything to wear for the party that they liked.

"Renée before we leave let's try to find a nice Hawaiian shirt for Keith. I went over to Ja'Ron's earlier in the week but he didn't have any Hawaiian print shirts."

With a raised eyebrow she asked, "Who is Ja'Ron?"

"Oh girl, he's one of Keith's good friends. They have known each other since college. He owns a clothing store in Detroit and he just opened another one in Ann Arbor a few weeks ago. I'm sure he'll be at the party. You'll meet him then."

"Oh, I didn't say I wanted to meet him. I just asked who he was since I've never heard you mention him before." Changing the subject Renée pointed ahead, "Maybe you'll find him a shirt in Neiman Marcus."

As they entered the men sportswear section in Neiman Marcus, Tiffany spotted the perfect shirt. "Thank God," Renée said to herself. She loved to shop but she hadn't walked the mall like this in a while.

"How do you like this one Renée?"

"I think it's perfect for Keith." It had been so long since she had even browsed through the men's department. Memories went back to when she would shop for the perfect clothing and cologne for Robert.

"Which color should I get?"

As if suddenly placed under a spell, she wondered if she would ever shop for any man again.

"Renée – Renée."

"Huh?"

"Girl, are you okay?"

"Yes, I'm just fine. What were you saying?"

"Which color should I get?" Tiffany asked.

"Um, the blue one would be my choice. The sunset in the background is beautiful. The palm trees look like they're blowing in the wind as the sailboats smoothly and calmly take over the water. Yeah Tiffany, that is definitely the shirt for him." Shortly afterward, they headed for a restaurant in the mall for lunch.

After eating lunch, they left the mall and went to the party store to purchase the invitations and decorations. They debated over which design to go with. The Luau print was a burst of lavish island blooms in assorted colors and the Tiki Luau would definitely set the tropical mood for the party. They finally decided to get the Tiki Luau design. For the centerpieces they purchased pineapples, parrots, crabs, lobsters, and palm trees. They purchased palm trees, flamingos, and Tiki Luau stirrers for the bar. They also bought tissue fruit straws. For the hostesses they purchased a few palm trees and parrot-designed plastic serving trays. They decided that they could add a nautical seaside exhibition with fish netting, mini rainbow fish, and various seashells in a section of the room. They both enjoyed planning parties. It was so much fun.

When Tiffany mentioned the costume store Renée hoped that she wasn't thinking what she thought she was thinking. Before she knew anything Tiffany handed her a coconut bra and a grass skirt to try on.

Lifting a brow Renée asked, "Tiffany who is this for?"

"It's for you silly," she said with a straight face.

"Girl, have you lost your mind? You know that there is no way I'm not wearing that. It is not that serious."

"Oh come on Renée, loosen up its just for fun. You can wear a pair of leggings underneath the skirt."

"Absolutely not! What are you trying to do? You know that's not my style."

"Renée chill girl, it's only a party. Come on we both know you have the shape to wear this, besides there will be other guest, with this stuff on."

"Like who?" she questioned with one hand on her hip.

"Nia and Regina has already informed me that they're wearing a halter-top with a grass skirt."

She chuckled. "You're kidding, right?"

"Do I look like I'm joking? You know they think they are the bomb. Both of them are definitely supermodel wanna be, and they love to dress like a hoochie."

"They are going to look a mess." They laughed at the thought of it. "Tiffany, whether Regina and Nia come to the party dressed like that or not I'm not comfortable with that. Are you wearing one?"

"I guess not. Come on let's get out of here." Tiffany threw her hands up, "Hold up Renée! I have an excellent idea. I can't believe I didn't think of it earlier."

"What is it Tiffany?"

"We are going to ride over to Patti's place."

"Tiffany, I'm not spending a whole lot of money on something I'll probably never wear again."

"Oh no, you won't have to. We'll have her whip up something nice and simple, and it's my treat."

What in the world had she gotten herself into? Off to Unique Designs they went. Renée knew something that was suppose to be small and simple would turn out to be a big ordeal. She began to try to think of which good excuse not to attend would work in her behalf. But, deep down inside she knew backing out would almost be impossible to do.

TWO

"Good morning daddy," shouted seven- year- old Jeremy as he jumped into bed with Ja'Ron.

"Hi there, how's my little tiger feeling this morning?"

"I'm doing great! Can you take me to the video arcade this weekend?"

Smiling and knowing what Jeremy would say next he replied, "I'll think about it." One, two, and three he counted to himself.

"Please - please dad."

Right on time he thought to himself as he began tickling the little guy. "Sure I'll take you to the arcade. We better get up now and get ready to begin our day."

"All right. Can I start picking out my own clothes to wear everyday?"

"Yes, I think you're old enough to coordinate your outfits."

"Yeah! I can't wait to tell Nana," Jeremy said excitingly.

"Make sure you pick out something warm to wear because the weather will be a little cooler today. I'm going to ask Marsha to drive you to school today because I have an early meeting to attend. Go ahead, get dressed and do your grooming so that you will have enough time to eat breakfast." As soon as Jeremy was dressed Ja'Ron heard him running downstairs calling Marsha , who he referred to as Nana.

"He is such a wonderful and happy kid." After selecting his attire for the day, he showered and began to get dressed. "Yeah, Jeremy is crazy about his Nana," Ja'Ron said aloud while smiling. She had just turned fifty-two a couple of weeks ago. She is about 5'4" and a little on the plump side. Her skin color is light with a few freckles on each cheek. Her long fine blend of sparkling gray hair is usually slicked back into a nice secured bun. She has never been married and she has no children. Whenever Ja'Ron and Jeremy go on vacation she goes with them.

"She's an absolute delight to be around and we love her dearly," he thought to himself as he continued to get dressed.

"Hi Nana!" shouted Jeremy as he ran toward her for his morning hug.

"Hello squirt how's Mr. Jeremy this morning?"

"Fine. Guess what?" Not waiting for her response he continued in a cheerful tone. "Dad said I could start picking out my own clothes to wear. How did I do today?"

"Go over and stand by the wall so I can check you out." He had on a pair of Sean John denim jeans, a Sean John shirt, and his Nike gym shoes. Smiling she said to him, "You go boy! If I were a little younger I'd give those little girls some competition. I think you did a wonderful job and you matched everything perfectly. Everyone knows that you are definitely a Moss."

Blushing like crazy Jeremy said, "Thanks Nana. I love you."

"You're welcome sweetheart and I love you more." Pulling out a chair for him she asked, "What would you like for breakfast this morning?"

"A bowl of Corn Pops please."

"One bowl of Corn Pops coming right up!"

"Good morning Marsha. How are you this morning?"

"Very well Ja'Ron and yourself?"

"I can't complain. Would you do me a favor by escorting Jeremy to school today? I know this is his last full week of school and I usually take him on Friday's but I have a meeting scheduled early this morning."

"Oh don't worry about it; I'll be more than happy to take him."

He kissed her cheek. "Thank you so much Marsha."

"Dad, are you picking me up from school today?"

"Yes sir, I'll be there. And then we're going out for pizza. How does that sound?"

Jeremy drank the last of his milk. "Cool."

Ja'Ron proceeded to his home office to grab his briefcase. As he began walking toward the front door Jeremy ran over to him.

"What's wrong buddy?"

Grinning he said, "I love you so much daddy."

Ja'Ron leaned down to give him a hug, "I love you too little tiger. I'll see you later this evening and have a good day okay."

"Dad, is Aunt Carla coming to visit us soon? I really miss her."

"I don't know when she will be able to visit us here again Jeremy. Did you forget that we are going to New York soon? Your summer vacation is beginning after next Wednesday and we'll be visiting her for a week so you'll see her then." He pinched his cheek.

"Oh Yeah!"

"I have to go now. Bye."

"Bye dad."

As Ja'Ron began the drive to his meeting he reflected back to when Jeremy came to live with him. Ja'Ron's parents were killed in a horrible car accident ten years ago. The man that hit their car was drunk which resulted in a head on collision. Everyone in the accident was killed. Losing both of them was very devastating to him and his sister. He was the oldest and Carla was five years younger.

His mom and dad adopted her when she was three months old. As soon as she was old enough to understand they told her that she had been adopted. She had no problem with it because she knew that they all loved her very much and she was taken care of very well. Actually, Carla was spoiled rotten. She never asked about her birth parents. As far as she was concerned the mom and dad who had raised her were the only parents she needed.

After their death, Carla moved to New York to pursue a career in modeling. Their mom had placed her in several pageants when she was very young. As she got older she began doing modeling assignments in the state of Michigan. Her mind was set to make it to the top in the modeling industry.

Standing 6'1", a slim and trim figure, that beautiful golden brown face, and that confident attitude she carried had definitely helped her to achieve her goal. She now graces the runways all over the world. She usually called Ja'Ron to tell him when she would be on television. He would make sure that they tune into the E channel or if they had plans, the VCR was set to tape the fashion show. Jeremy loved to watch his aunt strut down the runway in all of those fashionable clothing.

The only thing that Jeremy hated was when she wore the weird makeup. He would say, *"That makes her look very ugly when I know my auntie is pretty."* Ja'Ron would explain to him that she had to wear that because it's what the designer required. She was the most sought after model today and Ja'Ron was very proud of her.

Ja'Ron had spoken with her several times on the phone after the first couple of years since their parent's death, but he hadn't seen her. Anytime he mentioned his mom or dad she would instantly try to change the subject. He tried a few times to convince her to see a grief counselor. It had helped him to bring closure and to really accept their immediate death, but she refused. He figured one day she would have to deal with it and he would be there to help her.

The following year, right after New Year's Day, she called to ask him if she could come for a short visit and talk with him because she had a serious problem and she desperately needed his help. She would not give him any details or even a hint over the phone about what was troubling her. She said she would be arriving on Friday and she had to leave the following evening. She would rent a car and come straight over to his place.

He was thrilled at the idea of seeing her again. Whatever the problem was he knew it was resolvable. The doorbell rang and he was almost running to the door because he was so anxious to see her. She had finally arrived and still looked as beautiful as ever he thought, as he looked through the peephole. He opened the door, gave her a kiss on the cheek, and embraced her tightly.

As both of their faces flushed with joy he said, "Carla, I am so happy to see you."

"I'm happy to see you too big brother."

Ja'Ron didn't even notice that she wasn't alone until he heard a small cry. He glanced over to the side of Carla and there sat a baby carrier. His entire face dropped in shock. He was actually speechless. Thoughts began to swim around in his head. Was this her problem and if so what did she want him to do? He went from excited to extreme shock and confusion as he looked at the carrier.

She looked around and then over his shoulder. "So, can we come in?"

Ja'Ron was still dazed when he felt her shaking his arm. "Huh?" was all he could murmur out.

"Are you going to invite us in?"

Trying to get a grip on his emotions he scratched his head, "Oh, I'm sorry please excuse my manners. Come on in and make yourself comfortable. Would you like something to drink? Are you hungry?"

"No, I'm fine. Thanks anyway. Ja'Ron I want you to meet Jeremy. He's my three-month-old son."

Staring at her without a blink, "I know I didn't hear you correctly. Could you repeat what you just said? Whose kid is that?"

"He's my son and of course your nephew," she said as if discussing the weather.

Still sort of in shock, he didn't know if he should be happy or angry with her for not telling him that she had been pregnant. Didn't she know that he would have been there for her? Why did she hide this from him until now? There were so many unanswered questions. None of this made any sense.

"Ja'Ron in case you haven't already guessed, Jeremy is the reason for my coming here today."

Sarcastically speaking, "Oh I see, I haven't seen you for three years, and then you show up with a baby and expect me to be jumping for joy. Why didn't you tell me? What is wrong with you Carla?"

She sighed. "You have every right to be upset. I know I haven't been the greatest sister and I'm sorry for behaving in the manner I have been since…. You know."

"I know what Carla? Go ahead and just say it!"

She whispered, "Since mom and dad were killed."

"Don't you know that you were not the only person affected by the accident? We were supposed to be here for each other. Instead you chose to run away."

"I know Ja'Ron. I just couldn't remain in the same town any longer. I'm sorry that things didn't turn out differently. In my mind, it made sense for me to indulge my energy into pursuing my dream of modeling. So that's what I did. Look, I don't have a lot of time to spare here." Getting right to the point and not giving him anytime to digest all of this she said, "I need you to keep Jeremy for me for a while."

Both of his eyebrows shot up in surprise and his eyes widen. He paused for a moment and after taking a deep breath he shouted, "What! Have you lost your mind? Are you on drugs?" He started laughing.

She felt insulted and shouted back. "No I haven't lost my mind and no I'm not on drugs!" She paused as she attempted to calm down. "I thought I would be able to care for him while pursuing my career but I can't. I don't want him traveling all over the place and it doesn't make much sense for him to live with a nanny most of the time. You know that I'm hardly ever at home. I want him to stay with you until I am more settled."

"Where is his father?"

She turned her head to keep from facing him. "At the present time his father doesn't even know that he exists, and for now it is better that way. If the time ever comes, I'll deal with his father."

"What makes you think that I have time for a child right now Carla? Have you forgotten that I'm operating my clothing stores? I just opened a second store in Ann Arbor so I'm pretty busy myself. I don't have the time required to care for a child."

Watching her eyes fill with tears and desperately trying to reason she blurted, "That's just it Ja'Ron your business is well established and your life is more stable than mine is right now. You know if mom and dad were here, they would be more than happy to help me with him. Since they are not here, they would want you to support me."

"Don't you dare try sending me on a guilt trip," he grumbled while shaking his head.

"Please Ja'Ron," she begged as the tears rolled down her cheeks.

He couldn't believe this was happening. He didn't know anything about caring for a baby. "Somebody please pinch me and wake me up from this bad dream," he whispered.

Putting the pressure on Carla announced, "If you can't take him then I may have to put him up for adoption."

"What! Are you crazy? You have indeed lost your mind." Trying to control his temper he said, "I don't think you're in a position to make threats. Besides, I don't believe you would really do that or would you?"

"Don't force me to find out Ja'Ron," she pleaded.

"Carla, this is very selfish, not to mention manipulative. Where is my little sister? I want her back. This is unbelievable. Ever since we lost mom and dad you haven't been the same." He ran his hands over his face. Nothing could have prepared him for this.

"Life changes people Ja'Ron. I know I'm putting you in an awkward position, but I had no one else to turn to. I promise to come and see both of you as often as I can. Will you please take care of him?"

Deep down inside he knew that he couldn't turn his back on her. As long as he lived and until she married, he was responsible for her. He had to help her. While starring out the window, he threw his hands in the air and said, "Yes I'll take care of him. You know you really haven't given me much of a choice. By the way, how long is this for Carla?"

"To be honest Ja'Ron I don't know. I love you and I'm sure mom and dad is smiling down at you now for agreeing to do this. I am very grateful." She kissed him on the cheek and gave him a big hug. She picked little Jeremy up. "He's a really good baby. You'll fall in love with him quickly."

"Here, you want to hold him?" she asked as she handed the little guy over to Ja'Ron.

Taking a good look at him, he was golden brown in skin color; he had big pretty brown eyes with long eyelashes, and a head full of curly black hair. Jeremy looked up at Ja'Ron and he was smiling. He had very deep dimples in both cheeks.

"Isn't he beautiful? I think he looks a lot like you Ja'Ron."

Ja'Ron replied, "He is a handsome little guy."

"Jeremy's luggage is in the car. I need to give you some quick lessons on how to care for him."

After unloading the car he said to himself, "At least she didn't bring him to me without anything." She had three suitcases full of clothing, diapers, formula, et cetera.

She began instructing him on how to make his formula and how to change his diaper. He was a little slow changing his diaper because before he knew anything Jeremy was urinating all over the place.

Carla laughed while saying, "You can't play around when it comes to that."

"Oh no! This is not cool. I can't do this."

"Yes you can, and you will because you have no other choice."

Frowning at her Ja'Ron replied, "Don't push your luck Carla."

"Ja'Ron in the morning we'll go buy a crib and purchase other necessities for Jeremy." Jokingly she asked, "Will your business survive without you for about a week?"

He shrugged. "Yeah, I suppose it will."

"Good, I suggest you call and make arrangements because you will be very busy adjusting to your new life. You'll need to hire a nanny to watch him while you're not home. To begin with, I suggest you get a live in nanny until you get use to him."

He looked at her shaking his head. "You have everything all planned out, huh? I didn't know you were so inconsiderate of others. This is insane. Mom and dad would not be very pleased with you right now."

"Ja'Ron, I have no time to waste so just work with me okay. I don't want to fight with you the entire time that I'm here."

"Whatever Carla."

"And by the way, get a good night sleep tonight because when I leave tomorrow, until you have some help, your night or days will not be the same. I love you, good night Ja'Ron." She kissed his cheek. "You won't regret this, I promise."

"Good night Carla." Needless to say he didn't get much sleep at all. He tossed and turned most of the night. When he woke up the next morning he was hoping everything that happened on yesterday was only a dream. Then he heard Jeremy crying. "Reality check!" It was far from a dream. "What am I going to do? My life has been totally rearranged for me."

Inhaling deeply he decided that he'll have to make the best out of this situation. "Jeremy and I will be fine." He got dressed and after they ate breakfast they began their adventure for the day. They purchased baby furniture, a stroller, a different car seat, diapers, and formula.

Saturday evening before Carla left she instructed him to do two things on Monday morning: "Find a nanny and find a good physician." She left his shot records and an insurance card.

Ja'Ron was very thankful to have Keith and Tiffany as friends. Keith and Ja'Ron had been best friends since college. Although they could hardly believe what had happened they were very supportive and helpful with Jeremy especially during the first year. Tiffany was the one who help Ja'Ron choose the right nanny for Jeremy. Marsha had become part of the family. He didn't know how he would have survived without all three of them.

During the first year Ja'Ron had him, Carla managed to come once a month. After that year she couldn't come as often. Once Jeremy began talking he called Ja'Ron daddy and Carla insisted that he called her Aunt Carla. He questioned her about that. Her response was "Marsha is more like a mom to him than I am. Besides, I have an image to uphold." Ja'Ron decided it was best to just leave it alone. He didn't know what had gotten into her.

    Ja'Ron had to meet with Keith this morning at his law office. Not only were they best friends; he was also Ja'Ron's attorney. Keith and Tiffany once asked him about how he would feel if Carla ever decided that she wanted Jeremy back. At the time he was unsure of his feelings but lately, he had been giving it a lot of thought and he wanted him to remain with him. It had been over seven years now and Carla hadn't mentioned a word about him coming to live with her. Jeremy had never visited her without Ja'Ron or Marsha either. Ja'Ron really didn't think that she would ever want him back. She seemed comfortable with their arrangement.

    "Good morning Miranda. How are you on this gloomy day?"

    "Good morning Mr. Moss. I'm doing very well. Mr. Russell just arrived about ten minutes ago. I'll let him know that you're here. I just made a pot of coffee, so help yourself if you like."

    "Thanks, Miranda. I think I'll take you up on that offer."

Buzz. Buzz.

    "Yes, Miranda."

    "Mr. Moss is here to see you."

    "Thanks, you can send him right in."

    "Mr. Russell is waiting for you Mr. Moss."

    He nodded. "Thank you."

    "You're welcome."

    "Hey man, how are you?" Keith asked as they shook hands.

    "I'm doing good Keith."

    "How's my little man Jeremy doing?"

    "Oh he's fine. He's happy about life and is forever full of energy."

    "I'm happy to hear that. Have a seat and make yourself comfortable. So what's going on?"

He sighed as he sat down. "I've been thinking and I have decided that I'm going to ask Carla to give me custody of Jeremy. I've had him since he was a baby and a part of me would disappear if he ever left me. It's strange, but a lot of times I honestly feel like he is my natural son. Marsha once told me that was natural because of the length of time I have had him. Even though I know that he is not my natural son, I want him to legally be mine."

"Oh, I see." He stroked his chin. "Is it custody or legal guardianship that you want?"

"Whichever one Carla will agree to."

"Do you think that she will agree to either one of them? She might decide to take him away from you."

"To be honest I think that she will agree to at least legal guardianship. I don't think that she wants to be bothered with him for a long period of time. Don't get me wrong, she loves him dearly and would do anything for him. I just think that her career has been and still is more important to her. It's been over seven years now and she's never mentioned anything about him coming to live with her. Besides, since he's in school it would be in his best interest to remain in a more stable home since she's still traveling all over the world. So, I don't foresee her having a problem with me wanting him to legally be mine."

"What about his father?"

With a puzzled look he asked, "What about him?"

"Well he has rights and he will have to agree with you having guardianship over Jeremy."

"I hadn't thought about that. Actually, Carla has never told me anything about him. She did tell me when she brought Jeremy to me that the father didn't even know that he existed."

"To make matters even worse Jeremy doesn't know that Carla is his mom, and that I'm really his uncle. From the time he began talking she has insisted that he refer to her as Aunt Carla instead of mom. It didn't make much sense to me and I didn't push the issue too much with her. He has asked about his mom before. I told him that she was living outside the country." He shrugged.

"I hate lying to him but that answer has worked perfectly for now. I don't know what else I could say. Carla has really complicated all of our life and for what? A career that was more important."

"Selfish is more like it," Keith stated.

"Yeah, you're right. Let me talk to her and see what kind of information I can get out of her about his father."

"Man, this situation is a very unique one." He tilted his head and thought about the situation for a moment. "Yes, I suggest you talk with her about wanting guardianship over him before we go any further. You need to know how she is going to react to this. If she's agreeable then you'll have to press her about who and where Jeremy's father is. We don't want any problems later with the father, if he ever finds out about him."

"All right, I'm going to New York next week and I'm going to see Carla while I'm there. Actually we'll be attending some of her shows."

"Is Jeremy going?"

"Yeah, I'm taking him and Marsha. It'll be a nice vacation for all of us. We'll be there for a week."

"Good, you'll have a little time to think about everything and prepare for how you're going to present all of this to her. You're a good man. I don't think a lot of men would have taken on that kind of responsibility. Especially since he is not your child."

"He's family so I did what I needed to do. I just hope everything goes well with Carla."

"I'm sure it will." He slapped his hands together. "Ok, our business portion is officially over for now. Let's talk about the party that I believe you forgot to RSVP on."

Laughing Ja'Ron asked, "What party?"

"Yeah, you can play stupid all you want. I know you didn't think you were getting off that easy. If you hadn't come by today, I was going to contact you."

"Well, I didn't talk to Marsha to see if she had any plans for that night yet."

"You probably didn't plan on talking to her about it either did you? Well guess what buddy? You don't have to talk to her because I already did and she doesn't have any plans. The party is going to be a blast."

"Should I thank you or what?" he asked sarcastically.

"Don't worry about it. I just wanted to make sure you didn't have an excuse not to show up. Is there a special lady in your life yet?" He chuckled. "I guess what I'm really asking is if you will be bringing a date?"

"No, I haven't made the time for anyone lately. Every once in a while I might hang out with someone, no strings attached of course."

"You haven't seriously dated in almost a decade, huh?"

Frowning he replied, "As a matter of fact I haven't." He thought back to when he was actually serious about a woman. "Destiny was the last person I seriously dated. And man, am I happy that I let her go. I loved her, but didn't find the love I needed in return. The entire relationship was all about what she could get from me. I tried to work things out with her but I couldn't stand it any longer. Since Jeremy came to live with me all of my free time has been dedicated to him." He smiled whenever he thought about his little nephew. "Marsha is always telling me that Jeremy needs a mom around. I must admit lately I have been thinking about finding someone to settle down with. I just want someone who will truly love me for me, not what I can offer. Maybe someday I'll find that special person."

"You're never going to find her if you don't start mingling again."

"Good point."

"So you're coming right?"

"Yes, tell Tiffany I'm looking forward to it. It has indeed been a while."

"Don't forget, your attire should be something Hawaiian."

Waving his hand, "Yeah, yeah, you and Tiffany are such a trip. You're always coming up with something wild and crazy to do."

"Somebody's gotta do it. Besides, we just want to have fun with our friends and family."

As Ja'Ron stood to his feet he said, "All right man, I have to leave and go to work now."

"All right, I think I better do the same." He looked over at the huge file on his desk. "I'll see ya next Saturday. Tell Jeremy I'll be over to see him soon."

"He's going to be happy to hear that. I can see myself out. I'll check you later man."

"Later." Ja'Ron closed the door behind him.

With a devilish grin Keith murmured, "Little does he know. If Tiffany and my plans turn out the way that we think they should, you'll definitely meet that special someone real soon."

THREE

"Tiffany are you sure that Renée' is going to show up tonight?" asked Keith. "You know she might try to chicken out since this is her first outing in a while."

She shoved a piece of cantaloupe in her mouth. "Oh yeah she'll be here, even if I have to leave the party and go pick her up myself. But just to make sure she's here, I'll call and make up some reason for her to come earlier than everyone else. How's that?"

"That sounds good to me sweetheart. Do your thang girl."

"Baby, Ja'Ron is coming tonight isn't he?"

"Yes, he'll be here."

"Good. I'm going to call Renée now."

Ring… for the eighth time. " I know she's there. I hate I bought her that answering machine," Tiffany said as she tapped her nails on the counter. "Whatever Renée it's me, pick up the dog gone phone."

"Hello Tiffany."

"Hey Renée. I was just calling to see if you could come over early today. I need you to help me with a few things before the party."

"How early? I have had such a headache all day. Besides, I thought everything was ready Tiffany."

"Girl, just take a couple of Advil's and come on over. Don't forget your clothes. You can get dressed here. Can you be here by three o'clock?"

Glancing at the clock, it's already two o'clock Tiff." She sighed. "I guess so."

"Good, I'll see you then bye."

"Bye."

Renée knew what her friend was up to. "She isn't slick. That party doesn't start until seven tonight and I know that everything was completely set up on last night before I left", she continued. She knew that her friend was trying to make sure that she showed up. Smiling she said, "To reduce Tiffany's stress, I'll go ahead and get ready and head on over to her place."

The doorbell rang. Keith shouted, "I'll get the door honey." "Hello Keith, How are you?"

"I'm doing just fine Renée," Keith said while giving her a big hug. "I'm so happy that you decided to come tonight. You and Tiffany have done a great job with the setup for the party. I really like the exhibition. Check you out girl; I see that you have been taking good care of yourself." He hadn't seen her in a few months.

"Thank you for the wonderful compliment. A girl has to keep herself up, right? Besides that, your wife would have a fit if she thought that I was letting myself go."

He smirked. "You are so right about that."

"Where is Tiffany? She claimed she needed my help with something, but I know what she's up to. She didn't really think I would show up tonight did she?" They both laughed. "That girl is such a trip!"

"Well, you know your friend. She's has always tried to look out for you."

"I know, since the first day we met, she has always felt like she had to be my protector. Sometimes it's annoying though, I'm a big girl and I can take care of myself."

"She means well, and you know she considers you the sister that she never had. So everything she does is justified, in her book, because she cares so much about you."

"I feel the same way about her and we have been through a lot together. It may not sound like it, but I'm really not complaining because a lot of times I don't know what I would have done without her."

"I think you two have a wonderful relationship Renée."

"Yes we do, and I love the old gal no matter what she does."

"So how do you feel about the party tonight? I know that you have stayed away from events such as this since your divorce."

"I'm okay. And you're right it has been a long time, but I can't stay tucked in forever. I think it's about time for me to do something other than work."

"I agree. How is the business doing?"

"Business is wonderful and I am so thankful. It is truly a dream come true. It's been even better since Tiffany started the event planning with the business also. As soon as everything is finalized with the purchase of the new building we'll be well on our way.

"I'm so proud of you both. You two are going to be sucking in all of the money huh?"

"That's the plan," she said smiling.

As they entered the kitchen they found Tiffany busy putting out the floral napkins, "Renée I didn't know you already here."

"Keith and I were just having our chatting time."

"Oh, I see." She went over to the fridge and pulled out a large salad. Anyone want some?"

Keith looked over at her. "Honey, are you still eating?"

"Yep. Is that a problem?"

"Not at all, baby."

Attempting to catch her off guard Renée asked, "So what did you need help with Tiffany?"

Obviously surprised by the question Tiffany's face went blank, "Huh?"

Keith started laughing. "Well that's my cue to leave. I'll be in the den if you two need anything." Still laughing, he shook his head as he left the room.

"I knew you didn't really need any help. That's okay though, it was a good excuse to get me here early." Smirking at Tiffany she asked, "What time is the caterer coming?"

"They should be arriving any minute now. Let's just make sure we have everything else in place."

"All right girl, do you have the checklist?"

"I sure do. As soon as we're done we can get dressed for the party."

Aloha   Aloha   Aloha

    Renée stepped into the room and glanced around. The room was packed. There must be at least a hundred and fifty people at the party. People Renée hadn't seen in a long time had come. She greeted some of them as she approached her table. She was glad that Tiffany had one table reserved for them. Taking a seat, she spotted Tiffany doing her thing. Thinking of her best friend, "She has always been so outgoing. Sometimes I wish I had some of her spunk. Forget that, she has enough for the both of us."

    Renée began to further check out the room. "Tiffany was right about the grass skirts," she muttered. There were a lot of guests with them on. Most of them actually looked nice and wore them with taste. Ending that thought, she noticed Tiffany making her way over to their table.

    "Are you all right? What took you so long to join us? I thought I was going to have to come upstairs and drag you down here." She chuckled. "Just kidding. Come on with me and mingle. Don't you dare think that you're going to sit here all night."

    "I'm fine Tiffany, damn. You won't let me have any peace. I've only been sitting here for a few minutes. Just give me a minute and I'll start circulating."

    "I just want you to have a nice time tonight. Did you see Nia and Regina yet?"

    "No, where are they?"

    "They are on the other side of the room. I have to warn you now that they look like... well you'll see. Try not to be so obvious when you see them. Matter of fact grab a drink will ya?"

    "Oh boy... it's that bad huh?"

    "Yeah, they think they look good though. They both claim that they are going to find their dream man tonight." And I said to myself, "Not looking like that you won't. Girl, I'm so happy they didn't ask me how they looked. I don't know if I would have been able to lie with a straight face." They both laughed.

Bouncing his head to the beat, "This is a great party Keith. I'm glad I came."

"You can thank my lovely wife and her best friend for their excellent party planning."

Scanning the room someone suddenly caught his eye. "Say man, who is that woman sitting over there talking to Tiffany?"

Pretending at first not to see whom he was referring to, "I don't see Tiffany anywhere." Ja'Ron's face had a look of delight expressed all over it. He looked as if he had struck a gold mine. His expression was a good sign, Keith thought. "Where did you see Tiffany?"

"She's right over there." As he said that, the two got up from their seats. "Don't you see them standing now?" Ja'Ron moved so that he could get a closer look at her. "Gorgeous, gorgeous, gorgeous," was the first word that came to mind which would best describe this woman. Whoever she was, she was wearing the heck out of that dress.

"Yeah, that dress was definitely made just for her," he said aloud. It draped off one of her shoulder's exposing the length of her well- toned arms. The dress hugged every delicate curve on her body and the bottom of the dress flared out a little bit, which made her look even sexier. As she turned around he admired her beautiful black hair hanging down her back. *I hope it's not a weave.*" There were tropical Hawaiian flowers printed all over her dress and she had a flower tucked behind her ear. Continuing to look her over, he admired her toned legs relaxed in a sexy pair of sandals. She definitely has style, and her working out has indeed paid off. *She is beautiful, absolutely beautiful,"* he thought.

They had begun to walk around the room so he rejoined Keith. His eyes lit up as he asked Keith, "So are you going to tell me who that woman is or not?"

"Oh, I see them now. That's just Renée."

Repeating after him sarcastically, "Oh! That's just Renée. And... what does that mean?"

"She's Tiffany's best friend."

"If she is Tiffany's best friend, then why haven't I ever seen or heard of her before?"

"I'm sure you have seen her, you probably just don't remember."

"No way man, I would not have forgotten her."

"Well, she hasn't been out and about in a while. Now that I think about it neither have you." He smiled. "Anyway, she owns a Bridal Boutique here in Ann Arbor so she's been investing most of her time to that."

"In Ann Arbor huh?" *I'll get the exact location later.* "You know I can understand that. So what's the scoop on her? Is she married? Does she have any children? Not that having any children matters to me."

"Nope, she's been divorced for a few years now and there are no children."

He wondered, " What happened? Who in their right mind would let her go?"

Ja'Ron sat his drink on the bar counter. "Keith, I have to meet her tonight," he said in a desperate tone.

"Man, are you sure you can handle that?"

"Let me be the judge of that. You just get me an introduction tonight."

Keith said smiling, "No problem. Your wish is my command."

"Hi Nia and Regina, it's so good to see both of you again."

"It's good to see you too Renée," they both said. "Nia isn't that a beautiful dress Renée has on?"

"Yes, it is." Nonchalantly shrugging her shoulder, "Tiffany and Renée are always dressed to impress, so I'm not shocked. Where did you get that bad dress, Renée?"

"Unique Designs."

"Oh yeah, I should have known. That chick, Patti is the bomb. She's just too expensive for me," said Nia.

"How's the business?" Regina asked.

"The business is doing well."

"I heard you are planning to purchase that huge hall on Birch St. also."

"You heard right. Hopefully it'll be open for business real soon. Tiffany will be mostly running the hall though."

"Girl, you and Tiffany got it going on. We won't forget about y'all whenever we get engaged. Hopefully we'll meet the sucker tonight." Then they laughed.

"That's good to hear, thank you." Rolling her eyes and thinking to herself, *I really don't know about those two. They are something else. Tiffany and I have known them since high school and I don't know why or how we got stuck with them as associates.* Renée took a quick glance at their outfits and thought, *they have always taken fashion to a whole new level.*

Nia turned toward Tiffany. "Girl, you really know how to throw a party. Who set up the nautical seaside exhibition?"

"Renée and I did all the decorating ourselves."

"That was creative and everything looks great. And the food, of course, is off the hook."

"Thanks. Well, we need to keep circulating," said Tiffany. "We'll see y'all later and enjoy the party."

"For sure," they both said in unity.

They stopped at another table. As Renée stood there, she felt someone staring at her. Following the stare, she turned to a man who was standing by Keith. Her heart began to flutter from the intense glare. She suddenly felt breathless. She quickly turned her head back toward Tiffany. "Goodness, who is that guy and why is he looking at me as if I'm part of the entrée," she said to herself. She turned around again to sneak another peek at him but he was still looking her way. She suddenly felt butterflies dancing in her stomach. "This is not good," she said to herself.

"Renée, who were you looking at?"

Glancing over Tiffany's shoulder to avoid direct eye contact she replied, "Oh, I just thought I saw someone I knew."

"Yeah, I bet you did." She smirked. "Come on let's go check on Keith."

Attempting not to sound strained, "You go ahead, I'm going back to the table." She didn't want a close encounter with that guy. She wanted to avoid him if she possibly could.

She grabbed her by the arm. "Oh no, you're coming with me. There's someone I want you to meet. I see him over with Keith now."

"Oh my," she whispered as her heart began to beat faster. *Think of something quickly.* Hoping she wouldn't notice her anxiety, "Uh, Tiffany I... I need to go to the restroom. I'm going to the one upstairs, though."

"Ok, I'll be at the bar, so come over there before going back to the table."

"No problem," she frowned while lying to herself. She trotted up the stairs muttering, "Renée don't panic. It's not that serious. He probably thought you were someone he knew. Remain calm and cool, besides it's just a guy, don't sweat it." After putting on a fresh coat of lipstick, she returned to the party. As soon as she entered the room again, Tiffany waved for her to come over by the bar. The guy was standing with her and Keith watching every step she made. She continued to walk toward them, feeling as if the entire room was watching. It seemed as if every step had to be cautiously taken. His constant stare was making chills go up and down her spine. She had never had this feeling before. "I hate this. I really should have stayed home tonight," she muttered.

Ja'Ron could tell before even meeting her that this woman was "Classy." Watching her put one foot in front of the other was placing him totally under her spell. Watching her hips sway from side to side, she reminded him of a model who had mastered the runway. This feeling of love at first sight felt so right. As he continued to watch her approach them, he was determined to make her his woman.

Tiffany handled the introduction. "Renée Colby, I want you to meet Ja'Ron Moss."

Renée took a deep breath. "It's nice to meet you Mr. Moss," she extended her hand. His smile was very flirtatious. His teeth were almost perfectly straight and he had beautiful brown eyes. He was about 6'3" and his weight was well proportioned to his height. His complexion was a rich golden brown, and his goatee was perfectly shaped to his face. He was well groomed and she had to admit the man was fine.

"Aloha." His gaze went over her entire body. "The pleasure of meeting you is all mine Renée Colby." Her body began to tingle as he then lifted her hand to his mouth and gently kissed it. She suddenly felt an electrifying current rush through her body and she began to grit her teeth.

She thought to herself, *"So this is Ja'Ron Moss."* She didn't like the vibes that she was feeling from him. He was definitely breath taking, but she needed to remain focused. She didn't want this to be happening. Robert had done a number on her and she had to protect herself from being hurt by anyone else ever again. As she withdrew her hand from him, she smiled slightly at him. Tiffany and Keith watched them and smiled at each other.

Tiffany whispered to her, "You can stop gritting your teeth now."

Renée looked at her as if to say, "Is it that obvious?"

She then whispered, "Don't worry it's not that obvious I just know what you do when you become nervous. Loosen up, he's okay." Then the D.J. put on a slow jam.

"Would you like to dance, Renée?"

"Heck no, her mind screamed!" There was no way she wanted to slow dance with this fine, handsome man, and especially not to one of Luther's love songs. Being too close to him would be very dangerous. All she wanted to do at this moment was to find an easy escape from him. She opened her mouth to reject the offer and…

Tiffany quickly answered, "She would love to dance with you. Go ahead Renée and show him what you've got." She gently shoved Renée toward him. "Be careful out there, she's a wonderful dancer Ja'Ron."

Renée's eyes spoke sharply and clearly to her, "I'm going to kill you." Tiffany smiled and waved to her friend.

Ja'Ron grabbed her hand and escorted her to the dance floor. She glanced back at Tiffany and Keith and found her smiling like she had won a million dollars. Keith quickly hunched up his shoulders. *She is going to pay for this one; this time she has gone too far.* Renée wanted to wrap her hands around Tiffany's little neck right now and wipe that devilish grin off of her face.

"So Renée, how long have you known Tiffany?"

"Tiffany and I have known each other since kindergarten."

"Keith and I have been friends since college. I'm so surprised and disappointed that I hadn't met you before now. Life has a way of working itself out though. I guess this was our appointed time." He smiled. "Look, I don't mean to come on to you so strongly, but you are so beautiful. I would be honored if you allowed me the chance of learning more about you on a personal level." Not waiting for a response, he pulled her closer to him.

His body felt so right next to hers. *"Lord please restore my breathing and don't let me fall for this guy,"* she muttered. It had been so long since she had been this close to any man. She recognized the Armani cologne he was wearing and it was drawing her closer into him. Her entire body was burning from his touch. *Renée girl, keep your cool. Don't let him trap you like this. You have been through too much to let someone you just met creep in and intrude on your space.* She then responded to his request, "Right now I would rather not allow you or anyone else into my life. I'm so busy with my work and simply do not have the time for anything else." Some of it was indeed true, she tried to convince herself and she hoped that he would get the picture and leave her alone. Thank God the song had ended, he was making her sweat all over inside. She didn't like this feeling at all.

Leaving the dance floor he said to himself, "Yeah, she's the one, but I can tell she's not going to just openly come right to me.

She's tough and I'll have to wait patiently for her, but not too long though."

As they approached their table Ja'Ron leaned to whisper in her ear, "Well guess what, 'oh beautiful one'? Your answer was not good enough for me. And guess what else? I don't give up on what I want that easily." After pulling out her chair he spoke again, "I apologize if I am coming on a little strong, since we did just meet. However, I believe in voicing myself when necessary because you never know if the opportunity will ever present itself again." With that winning smile he continued, "Please don't leave the party before saying good night. Thank you for the lovely dance."

Giving him an annoying half smile, "You're welcome." He turned and walked away. Inhaling and exhaling slowly she muttered under her breath, "How dare him? Who does he think he is? He's got some nerves."

Startling Renée from behind, Tiffany leaned toward her and whispered, "The brother is fine isn't he Renée?"

Not now, she didn't feel like dealing with Tiffany. Giving her a scorching look she said, "Whatever Tiffany, you are so…"

"I love you too babe." While giggling she whispered, "Panties got a little moist huh? That's okay sweetie, you don't have to admit it now, and you can tell me all about it later." Teasingly she sang, "Renée's gonna get her groove back!" She laughed again.

She didn't need her humor right now. "You make me sick Tiffany. You had no right to just throw me out to that man like that. I really need to be mad with you right now." She frowned as she turned her head away from her. "You know, sometimes…"

"Oh, just shut it up. You know I can care less about you being mad 'cause we both know you'll get over it." Grinning she said, "You must admit he is fine, isn't he?"

She really wanted to wipe that grin off her face. "He's all right."

"Please girl, he is way beyond all right and you know it. You can tell somebody else that bull crap. And you know what else? I can see it all in your face that you're attracted to him. Don't be shy; I think that's wonderful. So tell me, did you give him your number?"

"Uh… no. Actually, I told him I wasn't interested in anyone right now."

"You did what? Are you crazy? Do you know how many women would jump at the chance to be with him? Look around here tonight; women have been drooling over him all night. When they saw you dancing with him they envied you because they wished it was one of them gliding all over the dance floor with him. As a matter of fact he hasn't danced or talked to anyone he didn't know besides you. Regina was trying hard to get some play, but he wasn't interested."

With a frown she blurted out, "So what Tiffany! Let the women jump. I'm sure he loves that anyway. He isn't *all that!*"

"Girl please that brotha is *FINE*, with all caps. I know him personally, and trust me what I do know about him he is all that and then some. Face reality girl, he ignited a spark in you tonight. Renée you have to come out of that shell and live again. You can't abandon love forever because of one mistake.

Watching Keith as he approached the table, she relaxed somewhat knowing that he was saving her from the total drill this time. Renée smiled at her and said, "Here comes Keith. Thank God."

"Tiffany, baby I need your assistance for a moment."

"Ok Keith, give me a minute and I'll be right there." Turning her attention back to her friend, "Renée don't move, I'm not done with you yet."

"Is that an order ma'am?"

"Take it however you want to. Just don't leave before I get back."

As soon as she left, Renée turned her head to the opposite side, and there he was pulling out a chair to sit next to her. Giving him a piercing, impolite, and irritating look she murmured under her breath, "Why me?"

Smiling Ja'Ron said, "Well gorgeous, are you ready to give me the right answer yet?"

Her body instantly stiffened. She had never met a man so blunt. "Which answer would that be Mr. Moss?" she asked with a slight attitude.

He placed one hand on her shoulder and said, "First of all you can relax your body. I'm not going to hurt you. Secondly, I would feel better if you called me Ja'Ron because I have every intention of referring to you by your first name." Moving closer to her he continued, "Thirdly, I would like the chance to get to know you better. Obviously you're not married because I don't see a ring on your finger. Furthermore, I don't think that you're involved with anyone because if you were he would be a fool to allow you out to a party, such as this, alone."

Shaking her head she murmured, "I don't believe this." He's got some nerves. If he were any closer he probably would have kissed her. He was creating feelings inside of her she hadn't felt before from anyone, not even Robert. Moving to put some space between them she said, "As I told you earlier, Mr. Moss – I mean Ja'Ron I am not interested. I'm a busy woman and I don't have much free time to offer anyone. So why don't you bark up someone else's tree? I'm not interested."

He took a sip of his drink before speaking again. "Renée you are so cold, but that's okay. And I know you probably want me to get out of your face right now and that's okay too. I can be a very patient man and I'm not going anywhere permanently. I don't know much about you but I can sense that someone has hurt you badly. All I'm asking for is a chance to show you lo.." Not wanting to scare her away, he paused choosing his words wisely, "life again. I'll give you a little time to think about it, and that's it. I'm a man who keeps his word so believe this; I'll be in touch with you real soon. Good night gorgeous." He kissed her on the cheek and left the table.

"Ooohhh", she grumbled. She hated the fact that he was intruding on her space. She hated it even more because she was attracted to him and he had been correct about her during his short observation. "I need to get up and outta here and that's exactly what I intend to do," she said to herself.

Tiffany came back to the table. "What's up girl? You look so preoccupied." Pinching Renée's cheek she asked, "Have you been hit by cupid's arrow? Your eyes are glistening. He got next to you didn't he? Somehow we knew that you two would be attracted to each other."

So this was all a set up. I should have known those two were up to something, she thought to herself. "Tiffany not now okay, I'm not in the mood. As a matter of fact, it's late and I'm tired so climbing into my bed is sounding really good right now. Standing to leave she continued, the party turned out great as usual, and I did enjoy myself."

"Did you really?"

"Yes, it was nice seeing people I hadn't seen in a while again."

"Ok girl, let's do lunch tomorrow and we'll talk then. I love you and thanks for everything."

"I love you too. Tell Keith I said good night." She gave Tiffany a hug and left the room. She pranced upstairs to gather her belongings. Before she reached the front door someone grabbed her arm. She gasped as she turned to see who it was.

"I'm sorry", replied Ja'Ron. "I didn't mean to startle you. You're leaving already."

"Yes, it's been a long day for me and I'm tired."

"I'm leaving also, so I'll walk you out to your car."

"Oh, that's not…"

He place a finger up to his mouth and whispered, "Shhh… I'm walking you out and that's it."

Turning to exit the house she whispered, "give me strength." After she got into her car, she thanked him for walking her out.

Before he shut her car door he blew her a kiss and said, "It was a pleasure meeting you this evening. I'm glad I decided to come. I'll be in touch real soon, Renée. Sleep tight."

As he climbed into bed Keith said, "Well baby, once again you threw a magnificent party."

"Thanks honey."

"I think this was the best party yet. A lot of the guests asked when the next themed party was being held. Someone even suggested that we throw a big masquerade ball next year."

"Yeah, this party was great and I couldn't have done it without my girl. A masquerade ball, huh? Renée and I would have too much fun planning that one."

"Speaking of Renée, did she enjoy herself?"

"She said she did. I think Ja'Ron might have struck a few nerves though. You know how stubborn she can be and you know how blunt he can be. This is going to be very interesting."

Keith smirked. "I did notice that they left out together."

Tiffany lifted a brow. "Really."

"Tiffany, I have never seen Ja'Ron so mesmerized. He monitored her like a watchdog. He took in every little detail about her. It was like watching a movie."

"Well, we kind of figured he would, right?"

"Right. He told me that he wants to develop a relationship with her and he knows that it's going to be a little difficult at first, but he's determined not to give up. He has already placed claim on her whether she likes it or not. He's convinced that he has to be firm with her because she is tough."

"Yeah, she is. I could tell that she's attracted to him, but you know how stubborn she can be. I think she is ready for a relationship, but she's just scared. You know she's like that because of Robert. We are having lunch tomorrow so I'll have a chance to see how she really feels. She's a successful businesswoman, the only thing she's missing is a good man. She's just trying to protect herself from being burned again."

"I still can't believe that low down mess he did to her."

"I tried to warn her, but she wouldn't listen. Anyway, she's too young to be so against loving again. I cannot and will not sit back and watch her be unhappy. I think that her and Ja'Ron would be good for each other. They both have been through so much over the past few years." She paused. "I know that deep down she wants to remarry and have children someday. I know Ja'Ron won't give up on her. Once Renée faces her fears, she'll realize that they are a perfect for each other. She'll thank us for bringing them together. There's no doubt in my mind about those two. They will be a happy couple." She yawned.

"Speaking of children, you want to work on that tonight?" He ran his hand across her cheek.

"Wait a minute, I have a present for you." She opened the chest drawer next to the bed and pulled out an envelope."

He gave her a puzzled look. He took the envelope and pulled the card out. On the outside of the card read, "Congratulations." Inside he read aloud what she had written:

You're going to be a daddy.
I can't wait to meet our new son or daughter.
Love your wife, Tiffany.

Then there was another paper attached to the other side of the card showing the positive results of her pregnancy test and the delivery date.

She smiled at him and gave him a tender kiss on the cheek before speaking. "I found out a week ago, but I decided not to tell you until after the party. It was very hard trying to keep it to myself."

His face beamed with joy, "I am so happy! Are you feeling okay? You haven't been sick have you? When is the next appointment?" After a short pause, "Thank God. I'm going to be a daddy. This is a wonderful gift. I Love You, Tiffany."

"I love you too, Keith."

FOUR

She opened the door for him and he immediately swept her into his arms. He lifted her chin and gently brushed his lips against hers. He hoped that she would willingly allow him entrance as he attempted to part her lips with his tongue. She parted her lips and he pulled her closer to him. He ran his hands throughout her hair and as their tongues entangled, he deepened the kiss. As he continued to seduce her with the intoxicating kiss he moved her slowly toward the bedroom. Keeping his eyes locked on her, he broke off the kiss to lift her onto the bed and began to unbutton her blouse. After removing her laced bra, he stared hungrily at her as he observed her well- rounded breast. As he lightly stroked each breast he said, "You are so beautiful." As he intensified the kiss once again his hands wandered all over her body. A low moan escaped her throat as he continued to explore every inch of her. "You are an angel designed just for me. I promise you that I'll never hurt you, just give us the chance that we deserve," he whispered.

"Mmmm…" His gentle touch was making her blaze all over. Never in her life had any man made her feel so good. This man had a magical touch and she didn't want it to ever end.

He said in a deep seductive tone, "I need for you to understand that once we do this there is no turning back. We will belong to each other. I love you Renée. Are you ready to commit?"

Renée sat straight up in her bed! She was struggling to catch her breath. Looking around the room she realized she was alone. It was only a dream. She had been dreaming about Ja'Ron. She brought a hand up to her chest. "What is happening to me?" The dreamed seemed so real. "Girl, you are in serious trouble." She inhaled and exhaled slowly. She really didn't want to think about what this could mean. Ja'Ron had made himself very clear about his intentions. This was very disturbing to her. The thought of him making love to her was sending tremors throughout her body.

Staring at the ceiling she asked herself, "Am I honestly ready for a relationship?" Truth being told, Tiffany was right about her not wanting to go through life alone. She knew she wanted to be married again and to have children someday, but she was so afraid of being hurt again. Robert's affair had hurt her deeply. She just wasn't sure if she was willing to take a gamble on love again. She was definitely attracted to Ja'Ron. How was she going to deal with this? "I'll feel better after a nice hot bubble bath." She got up to run her a bath.

As she relaxed in her Jacuzzi, she began to reflect on the cause of her divorce. Renée and Robert were a very happy couple once. They had dreams of having a family someday. After three years of marriage they had decided that they would try to have a baby. It took about six months of trying before she found out she was pregnant. They were so happy about the baby until the day she had a miscarriage. Ever since that happened, he began acting differently toward her. He worked all the time. When she complained about him not spending any time with her he claimed that he was too tired to do anything with her.

Her cousin Mya had come to live with them shortly after Renée found out she was pregnant. She had just turned twenty-three and she was attending the University of Michigan to finish her master's degree. Tiffany was always making negative remarks about her. She didn't trust her, not one little bit. Furthermore, she advised Renée to get her out of her house before disaster struck. Mya was family, and being that tuition was high enough Renée wanted to help her as much as she could. She blew off Tiffany's concerns because Mya hadn't given her any reason to put her out.

After the miscarriage Renée became really depressed, and Robert's attitude didn't make matters any better. Although she knew losing the baby wasn't her fault, she felt as if he was blaming her and was punishing her dearly. He offered her no comfort at all. If Tiffany had not been there for her she didn't know how she would have survived.

A few weeks passed and Tiffany insisted on her getting out of the house. Renée told Robert that her and Tiffany were going on a shopping spree out of town and she probably wouldn't be back home until the next day. He gave her a kiss on the cheek and told her that she probably needed an overnight getaway and to have a nice time.

Renée and Tiffany did a lot of shopping that day. Instead of having an overnight stay they decided to return home after dinner. As Tiffany pulled into the driveway, Renée noticed Mya's car was home. She thought it was kind of strange since she had late classes on that particular night, but chose not to say anything. They both looked at each other and Renée knew that it would be hopeless to believe that Tiffany would keep quiet. She couldn't help but wonder why Mya was home herself.

Tiffany pasted a big frown on her face. "Renée, I thought Mya had late classes tonight."

She shrugged her shoulders. "She does, I guess she got out early."

Tiffany rolled her eyes at Renée and the tone in her voice sounded irritated. "Maybe she did. Come on, I'll help you carry your bags in."

Renée's body suddenly felt jittery. Something just didn't feel right. She opened the door and called Mya's name and no one answered. Then she walked toward the garage and noticed Robert's car was also home. She called out Robert's name, again no answer. Trying not to sound worried she told Tiffany that he was probably in his study sleeping and maybe she was out with one of her friends.

Tiffany placed one hand on her hip and sighed. "Let's take your bags up to the guest room." They proceeded to go upstairs. As they reached the top of the stairs, they could hear a female's voice moaning. For a brief moment Renée closed her eyes.

"What in the world?" Tiffany asked.

Then they heard the male's voice moaning. "Mmmm… Ooohhh baby… I love you."

As Renée turned toward Tiffany she identified the male's voice, "That's Robert."

Renée placed one hand on her chest and froze in her spot, "Oh dear God no, this is not happening," she managed to say. She suddenly felt faint.

Tiffany dropped the bags and grabbed Renée so that she wouldn't fall. "Come on Renée you have to do this, open the bedroom door. If you can't open it, then I will." They walked to the bedroom door.

Tears filled her eyes and she trembled as she turned the doorknob. She threw one hand over her mouth and her pupils dilated as she stood there watching her husband and her cousin make love. Nothing could have prepared her for this scene unfolding before her eyes. She slowly walked over to the bed. Her heart was beating fast. They didn't even know that anyone was in the room until Renée angrily yanked the covers off of them and screamed out "Nooooo! How dare you do this to me! Get out… both of you ….GET OUT!" They both jumped, looking astonished to see Renée there. Renée began to yell. "What's the matter Robert? You didn't think I was coming home tonight? Get out and take your slut with you." Renée fell to the floor, covered her face and cried. She felt like her life was completely over now. How was she ever going to recover from this?

She had almost forgotten that Tiffany was there until she felt her put her arms around her and whisper, "I am so sorry Renée. You didn't deserve this. He is going to pay dearly for hurting you like this." She then left the room, and she could hear Tiffany and Robert arguing. Shortly afterward, Tiffany returned to the room and sat next to Renée. "You are strong Renée and this will take some time but you know that I'll be here for you. I'm taking you home with me for a few days. I'll help you pack a few things."

After releasing an exasperating sigh, she gave Tiffany a hug and said, "Thanks." Renée handed Tiffany some more things to put into her overnight bag.

Mya peeked into the room. "I am so sorry, I really didn't mean for this to happen.

Renée walked into the master bathroom to retrieve some personal items. She didn't respond to Mya, and then she heard Tiffany slap her across the face. *"GET OUT!"* Tiffany screamed out.

"It served her right," Renée murmured as she grabbed her make-up bag.

Tiffany continued talking to Mya. "After everything Renée has done for you, was this your idea of repayment? I never trusted or liked you anyway. I knew you were going to be trouble. You better not ever come near Renée again." Mya lowered her head and exited the room.

Robert tried desperately to patch things up with Renée so that he could move back home. He knew he had a good wife; he just didn't appreciate her like a husband should. But a few months later he told Renée that Mya was pregnant with his child. He confessed that the affair had been going on before Mya ever came to live with them. That's when Renée filed for divorce. It was time for her to move forward with her life. It took some time but she did forgive Robert for hurting her. She also dared herself not to love again because she couldn't afford another heartbreak.

Tiffany and Renée pulled into Red Lobster's parking lot at the same time. They went inside and were immediately seated, which was unusual for a Sunday.

"You appear to be a little tense today, Renée. What's going on?"

She shrugged. "I think that I'm just a little tired from last night, that's all."

"Did you rest well?"

"Not really. I tossed and turned most of the night."

"Thanks for helping with the party. Everyone seemed to have enjoyed themselves."

"You're welcome."

"Speaking of last night, what did you think about Ja'Ron? Did you like him?"

Who in their right mind wouldn't have? she thought but instead decided to say, "He's not my type."

"You don't even know him. I'm sure you know that he's very interested in you but I'm sure you were trying your best to shoo him away. Am I correct?"

"You're right, but I think the timing is off because I'm simply not ready." She focused her attention on a painting hanging behind Tiffany.

"Will the timing ever be right with you? You can't let what Robert did to you ruin your entire life. You have to move on with your life." Frowning she said, "I never liked him anyway. He was never good enough for you as far as I was concerned. I just tolerated him because of you."

Renée lifted a brow as she turned her full attention back to Tiffany. "I never knew you didn't like him."

"I didn't say anything because I could see that you loved him so much. I guess I was trying not to judge him too harshly. But I did feel like you contributed more to your relationship than he did. I'm not saying that he didn't make you happy for a while but you know that everything was all about him. I know it's unusual but I managed not to speak badly of him to you."

"When has that ever stopped you?" They both laughed.

"All that mattered to me was that he treated you right and that you were happy. He's old news and I've wasted enough breath on him. Anyways, you're young, beautiful, and you have to let the past go in order to move on with your life."

"If I move on that would mean I would have to love and trust again and I'm not quite sure I can do that yet." She still had that hurt look in eyes. Tiffany wished she could take away the pain.

Tiffany reached over to touch her hand. "Well you'll never know until you make that first step. Ja'Ron is a wonderful guy. All I'm asking is that you give him a chance."

"Why is a nice looking man such as Ja'Ron single? I know he probably has women crawling all around him. And he's most likely a heartbreaker too. I just can't afford to get involved with someone like that. I have to protect myself."

"Don't be so quick to judge. As a matter of fact, you've got it all wrong. He is not a womanizer or a playboy at all. He has been spending most of his time building his business. I'm sure you of all people can understand that. Yes, women would love to have him not only because of his looks but also because he's a very successful man. He may have friends that he hangs out with sometime but as far as I know he hasn't seriously dated in over seven years. His parents are deceased and he has one sister who is a supermodel and also very selfish. Over seven years ago she basically dropped her son off on him to take care of. His time has been devoted to his business and more so to his nephew Jeremy." She paused for a few moments. "Do you remember the time when I told you I was helping one of Keith's friends with his nephew?"

"Now that you mention it, I do remember that."

"Well that's him. He is an honest and responsible man. Furthermore, I think that the both of you would be excellent for each other. Don't you want to be happy again? I know you want to be married and have children, right?"

"Yes I do, but I don't want to be hurt again."

"All I can say is to just take it one day at a time and see what happens. Hey, before I forget, is everything all set for our trip to New York?"

"Yes, all of our reservations have been confirmed."

"We'll be gone for a week right? And what hotel are we staying at?"

"One week is correct and we'll be staying at the Waldorf Astoria. You made the reservations, don't you remember?"

"I was just making sure you didn't change anything. She smiled and kissed Renée's cheek. This will be a nice vacation for both of us. It's been a while since we vacationed together."

FIVE

"Daddy, when are we going to see Aunt Carla?"

"We'll see her on tomorrow Jeremy. We're going to see her at the show and then you're going to spend the night with her. How does that sound?"

"I can't wait! I'm going to bed early so that tomorrow will hurry up and come."

"All right buddy. Good night." He tossed and turned all night thinking about Renée. He wanted to see her again soon. The dance they shared was replayed in his dreams. She was a smooth dancer. He decided that as soon as he got back to Detroit he would contact her.

"Renée, did you make out an agenda for the week?" Tiffany chuckled.

"Tiffany, I told you that we didn't need an agenda. After the bridal show, we are free to do whatever we want to do. This week is going to be a busy week of shopping and whatever else we choose to do."

Tiffany hunched her shoulders up as she finished placing her clothing in the drawers. "Well you're the one who always have to have everything planned out."

Renée placed her make-up bag and perfume on the bathroom counter. "Not this time girlfriend. The show is only for a day and after that we're going to have fun." What Renée didn't know was that Tiffany had an agenda of her own planned just for her. She smiled as she thought about her surprise.

"Tiffany, I'm going to shower and go to bed because I'm tired from the flight."

"Ok. I'm going down to the ice machine, I'll be right back." She went into the ice room and as she turned to leave she spotted Ja'Ron and Jeremy. She quickly jumped back into the little room, hoping they didn't see her. After a few minutes had passed she peeked out to make sure that the coast was clear. "Oh boy, now that was close." She hurried back to the room and realized she had left the ice container. "Here I go again." She hurried back to the ice room and arrived back to the room without being caught. "Whew." Renée was still in the shower so she decided to call Keith to let him know that they had made it to New York safely. She also wanted to let him know that she had seen Ja'Ron.

"Tiffany hurry up, I don't want to be late for the bridal show." She had been in the bathroom entirely too long. "Girl, what are you in there doing? I believe if it were up to you, you would be late for your own funeral." Renée chuckled as she threw her head back over the chair.

Tiffany opened the door and her face looked a little pale. "Give me a break Renée. We have plenty of time to make it to the show. I just need to put on my lipstick and I'll be ready." She moved slowly toward the bed.

"Wait a minute, Tiffany. Something's wrong. Are you okay?"

"Yes, I'm fine. Why?"

"Your face looks a little pale that's all."

"I'll be ready in a minute. I forgot to put on my lipstick." She returned to the bathroom. She turned on the water so that Renée couldn't hear her. She was not feeling too well. She just needed a few more minutes to pull herself together."

Five more minutes passed by. "Geez, it doesn't take that long to put on lipstick and why does she have the door closed for that. Something isn't right." Renée knocked on the bathroom door. "Tiffany are you okay?"

Tiffany opened the door and embraced Renée. "Help me over to the bed. I need to lie down for a few minutes." She let out an exasperating sigh. " I have something to tell you."

"What's wrong Tiffany? Tell me what is going on with you," she demanded.

" Nothing's wrong. Everything is so perfect. She then began to smile. How would you like the idea of becoming a godmother soon?"

Renée bit down on her lower lip. "What are you trying to tell me Tiffany?"

"I'm pregnant. I'm about eight weeks now."

Renée's eyes filled with tears of joy as she grabbed Tiffany and hugged her. "This is exciting news. I would be honored to become a godmother. So, you're feeling a little sick, huh?"

"Yeah, I'll be okay once I eat something." She reached over and grabbed some crackers to help settle her stomach. After lying there for a few more minutes she said, "Come on, I'm ready now, let's go."

"Are you sure you're all right? If you don't feel like going to the show, it's okay. You know you'll have to take it easy for a while, right? I don't want you to over do things."

"Yes ma'am. I'm fine now and I promise to take it easy. You and my husband will have to remember that I'm pregnant not handicapped."

"Ok. When we get to the show you can eat something more solid there." The bridal show was being held at a hotel down the street from where they were staying.

After they picked up their materials from the registration table they entered the room to find a seat. Renée was happy because they found an empty table in front of the runway. They had about twenty minutes to spare before the show started. Tiffany decided to go to the restroom. Afterward, they got something to eat and drink before returning to their seats again. Shortly after taking their seats, a cute little boy who obviously knew Tiffany ran over to where they were. She gave him a big kiss and a big hug. Without introducing the child, she said to Renée, "I'll be right back," then she walked away with him.

Renée wondered, who was this kid, where was his parents, and how did Tiffany know him? Then she noticed an attractive older lady approach Tiffany and they greeted each other. Renée figured it was probably his grandmother. "Oh well." She continued to eat her food but something didn't make sense. She suddenly had an uneasy feeling. "Why did Tiffany take off like she did?" She shrugged her shoulders. "I guess if she wants me to know them she'll bring them over to the table and introduce them."

"Now, where did those two run off to?" Ja'Ron began to scan the room. "I don't believe my eyes. Is that her? Naw, it can't be." Then he spotted Marsha. Moving closer to where Jeremy and Marsha were standing, he noticed them talking to Tiffany. He became curious. "What was Tiffany doing here? Was Keith here somewhere?" He shook his head as he tried to remember if Keith mentioned anything about coming to New York. Strangely, he felt a need to continue to search the room, not really knowing who or what he was looking for. He suddenly made contact to the area where he thought he had seen a familiar face. Deciding not to go over to where Marsha and Tiffany stood chatting he headed over to where he thought he saw Tiffany's best friend. He whispered, "That's it… maybe Tiffany was here with Renée."

Once again Renée felt uneasy. It felt like someone was staring at her. Then she shrugged off the idea and thought that it was probably Tiffany. Not turning to look around, she continued to eat.

Approaching her with a wide smile, "Well knock me off of my feet, is that really you Ms. Renée Colby? This must be my lucky day."

That deep sexy voice was unforgettable. Almost choking, she managed to look up to see him smiling. It was Ja'Ron Moss. "For goodness sake, what is he doing here?" she muttered. She gave him a polite smile. He was wearing a navy blue Sean John suit. She was happy to see him and dang he most certainly looked good she thought to herself.

"What a pleasant surprise. Good afternoon, Renée."

Breathe girl. "Good afternoon, Mr. – I mean Ja'Ron. What are you doing here?"

"I was about to ask you the same question," he said as he sat down next to her.

She cleared her throat before speaking again. "I'm in the bridal business, therefore, I rarely miss a good bridal show especially in New York. I have to keep up on what's in and what's out. So, what are you doing here?"

"It looks like we have something in common. I own a clothing boutique, so I attend fashion shows throughout the year also. Although bridal gowns are not my specialty, I am here because my sister is a model and she just so happens to be in this particular show. He quickly changed the subject. "I couldn't help but notice that we chose the same color to wear today. You look stunning."

Until he mentioned it, she hadn't noticed that they had on the same color. She was wearing a navy blue pants suit. "Thank you, I guess we are wearing the same color."

Tiffany, along with the lady and the cute little boy returned to the table.

"Daddy, look whose here?" Ja'Ron stood to greet Tiffany.

"I see. He kissed her on the cheek and gave her a hug. Tiffany I didn't know you were going to be in New York."

"Oh, Keith didn't tell you?"

"No, he didn't mention you coming here at all."

"It must have slipped his mind." She smirked quietly.

"Probably so, Renée, please excuse my rudeness. Let me introduce you to my family. This fine young woman is my surrogate mom Marsha Clay, and this handsome little guy is my son Jeremy. Marsha and Jeremy I would like for you to meet Ms. Renée Colby."

The well groomed lady extended her hand and said, "It's so nice to finally meet you."

Renée wondered, what did she mean by that? Had he been talking about her to his family? She replied, "It's nice to meet you also Ms. Clay."

"Calling me Marsha would be fine."

"I'll remember that, and you can call me Renée."

As she extended her hand to Jeremy, he shocked her by taking her hand and delivering a kiss on it. "It's a pleasure to meet you Ms. Renée."

The cutie was just as charming as his dad. "It's a pleasure to meet you to Mr. Jeremy."

"You can call me Jeremy if you like."

"I would love that and you can call me Renée okay."

"If you all don't have a table yet, please feel free to join us." Tiffany quickly offered.

"Thanks, we'll take you up on that offer," Ja'Ron said as he pulled out chairs for the women and then for Jeremy.

Tiffany asked Ja'Ron, "So what are you doing here?"

"Carla is in this show. I can't believe Keith didn't tell you that I would be in New York this week. He knew weeks ago that I was coming here."

With a lifted brow Renée turned to look at her while she answered. She had a funny feeling that her friend had been scheming once again.

Trying to look innocent she said, "No, I don't recall Keith mentioning it at all." She raised her glass to take a drink from it.

"So, how long are you ladies staying in New York and where are you staying?"

Tiffany was more than happy to answer him. "We are going to be here all week also and we're staying at the Waldorf Astoria."

"What a coincidence, that's where we're staying," Ja'Ron announced with a wide grin. Ja'Ron and Renée made eye contact. He wanted to reach out and touch her. She quickly turned her head. He smiled. *A man couldn't have any better luck.* His thoughts of getting closer to her began to escalate. He wanted to everything there was to know about her.

Renée couldn't believe her ears! She wanted to sink all the way down into her seat. How was she going to handle being under the same roof, *so to speak*, as this charming man? It may have been coincidental that they were at the same show, but she was sure that the hotel arrangements were not. Tiffany had insisted on making the air and hotel arrangements. She had to admit the girl was clever and was much better at this kind of stuff than she.

Renée thought about the day they had eaten at Red Lobster. It was making perfect sense now. That's why Tiffany questioned her about the hotel and the length of stay. She wanted to make sure Renée hadn't changed any of her plans. "That scheming little witch!" Renée muttered under her breath. Renée looked at Tiffany and shook her head. She knew that Renée had figured it all out. All Tiffany could do was shrug her shoulders up and smile.

After the show was over, Ja'Ron introduced his sister Carla to Renée. Jeremy was so happy to see Carla, but Renée wondered why he was calling her Aunt Carla instead of mom. Come to think of it Jeremy called Ja'Ron daddy, and he introduced him as his son. This was confusing. What was really going on? "Oh well, it's none of my business anyway," she muttered.

Carla turned to her brother and said, "She's beautiful. Go for it big brother, she already has my approval. First impressions means a lot."

Renée pretended not to hear what she said to Ja'Ron. Then Carla invited her and Tiffany to her place for dinner before the week was over. Carla, Marsha, and Jeremy said good night and left.

Tiffany chuckled and then whispered to Renée, "I'll say they all liked you. I knew they would." All Renée could do was glare at her friend, she was speechless.

"Ja'Ron we should have dinner together, if your schedule will allow it." Tiffany announced.

This chick never gives up. "Tiffany, I'm sure he's going to be busy and so are we. It was nice seeing you again Ja'Ron. I hope your stay in New York will be pleasant."

"Thank you, I intend for it to be even more pleasant now that I know that you're here." Giving Renée a seductive smile he continued, "I would love to take you two out to dinner one night. How about tomorrow evening? Marsha and Jeremy will be spending the day with Carla. I'll call Marsha to let her know that I'll be joining you ladies for dinner tomorrow evening."

"What time will Marsha and Jeremy be back at the hotel?"

"I don't know. Why?"

Renée didn't like the direction that she knew her friend was headed toward. She let out a small sigh and looked at Tiffany, but she wouldn't look her way. "Here we go," Renée whispered. It was no point in her saying anything. When it came down to this sort of stuff she couldn't beat Tiffany at her own game.

"I was just thinking that maybe you and Renée could go out to dinner and I'll keep myself busy until Marsha and Jeremy return and then I'll hang out with them."

Renée quickly spoke up hoping it would work this time. "That's not necessary. I'm not leaving you alone, especially in your condition."

"I'll be fine Renée, just chill."

Ja'Ron curiously asked, "What condition?"

"Keith and I are expecting our first child."

"Wow, that's great. Are you sure you'll be okay?"

"Not you too. Come on y'all, I'm only pregnant. I'll be fine." Turning to Renée she said, "Ja'Ron tell Marsha to call the room when she returns tomorrow." She then winked at Renée.

"Alright. What room number are you in?"

"We're in room 511."

Ja'Ron smiled "We're on the same floor. I'm in room 513 and Marsha is in room 517."

Renée brought her hand up to her chin and shook her head in disbelief. How did Tiffany manage to get rooms on the same dog gone floor? There is no way of escaping this man. I guess going out to dinner with him wouldn't hurt anything. Maybe then he would leave me alone.

"I have one more show to attend on tomorrow afternoon. I should be back at the hotel around four. Is six o'clock okay with you Renée?"

"Sure, I'll be ready by then." Tiffany winked at her and smiled.

"Well if you ladies are ready to leave, please allow me to escort you back to the hotel."

"Thank you," they both said.

Renée and Tiffany spent most of the next day shopping at various shops in Manhattan. They noticed it was getting close to three o'clock so they decided to head back to the hotel. Besides, Tiffany wanted to make sure her friend had plenty of time to prepare for her date.

"Renée, why don't you wear that dress you bought today? I think that would be perfect for the occasion."

She moved the plastic from the dress. "Maybe you're right. I'm glad I bought some shoes to go with it today too." After figuring out what to wear she began to prepare for her date. "Do you think he will like this dress Tiffany?"

Tiffany threw her hand up and waved. "Girl, please. Trust me he'll like it. I'll help you with your hair once you finish dressing."

SIX

Ja'Ron sighed as he gave Renée an approving look. "Wow… you look beautiful." She wore a sexy black and red form fitted dress, which revealed a little cleavage, just enough to make the mind wonder. The black sandals, in which buckled at the ankle finished setting the attire off. Her hair was pulled back off her face and her makeup was perfect. "It looks like we are color coordinated again. I like that."

He was dressed in a black suit, and wore a red and black designed tie. "Well, you look nice yourself. It is strange that we have worn the same colors twice in a row. Pure coincidental."

"I made reservations for us, I hope you enjoy the restaurant I selected."

She smiled. "I'm sure it'll be fine." There was a Mercedes limo waiting outside for them. Inside was a beautiful bouquet of roses. "Wow," she muttered.

The restaurant was absolutely gorgeous. The greeters escorted them pass several vacant tables and she couldn't help but wonder why they had passed them all up. She also noticed there were no reserved seating signs on them. Then they walked up a flight of stairs. Where on earth are we headed to, she wondered. He had reserved a private room and there were candles lit everywhere. The room was very cozy and romantic. Renée inhaled and exhaled deeply as they were seated at their table. Violin players shortly joined them, playing soft music. *Ja'Ron definitely knew how to make a good impression,* she thought. The waiter returned with their drink selection. After taking a few minutes to scan the menu, they both ordered a Marinated Octopus Salad with Roasted Tomato Coulis, Red Wine Vinegar and Sea Snail. For the main meal, she ordered Steamed Maine Lobster with Whole Braised Fennel and Basil Broth and he ordered Grilled Rabbit with Asparagus, Cauliflower Mushrooms and Whipped Potatoes.

"How's your food?"

"It's great, this restaurant is exquisite."

"Good. I'm glad you like it."

"So tell me something about yourself Renée."

She shifted in her seat before speaking. "What is it you want to know?"

"There's a lot I want to know." He chuckled as he curiously watched her. "Let's start with what made you get into the bridal business."

She smiled at this question because it brought her such joy to talk about her business. "I always knew as a teenager that I would own a bridal boutique. My mom directed weddings part time, so I accompanied her most of the time. As the attendants marched in, I would take note of what they wore from head to toe. I always had a notebook handy and I wrote down any mistakes the bride made coordinating their attire, such as, wearing the wrong type of shoes, the wrong accessories, etc. I hated it even more if the hairstyle didn't compliment the gown being worn."

She paused for a moment to drink some water. "After each wedding I would talk to my mom about what I would have done differently. She was fascinated at how much attention I paid to the affair. She also adored my sense of style." Her eyes were gleaming. "At the age of sixteen, I remember telling my mom that I wanted to own a bridal boutique. Not only would I sell bridal gowns and dresses for the wedding party but I would also assist the bride in coordinating their attire from their earrings down to the shoes. If something would not look good together I would advise them on what would be more appropriate. Of course, the final decision would be up to the bride."

She shifted in her chair. " I also wanted my place to be a one stop shop, so my goal was to carry shoes, gloves, hosiery, earrings, etc. If I didn't have the item on the sales floor it could be ordered. In addition to that, I'll soon own a place where weddings and receptions can be held in the same place. I'm really excited about that." She suddenly got really quiet.

He noticed her mood change and asked, "What is it Renée?"

She glanced away from him as her eyes began to fill with water. "My only wish was that my mom had lived to see how successful I am today." She fought to hold back the tears. He placed his hand on top of hers. She felt the heat pass through them and as if suddenly hypnotized they both gazed at each other. She broke the trance by moving her hand. "I apologize, I didn't mean to get all sensitive."

"It's okay, there's no reason for an apology. I understand. I'm sure you have made her proud. Is your father still living?"

She sighed. "No, he died when I was three. The only memories I have are the one's my mom shared with me. There were a couple of videos of us all together, and a few photos."

"Oh, I'm sorry to hear that and believe me I do understand. I lost my parents some years ago. They were involved in a fatal car accident. So I understand what it's like not to have your parents around. I was the only biological child and my sister Carla was adopted later once my parents found out they couldn't have any more children. We were a very close family. I always adored fashion also, that's why I ended up owning my own boutique."

She felt at ease talking to him and she had to admit she was having a great time with him. After dinner they decided to go dancing at a nearby club. "What a evening," Ja'Ron said as he moved closer to Renée in the limo. "I really enjoyed myself tonight and I want to spend more time with you. How would you feel about that?"

She thought to herself, he is absolutely gorgeous. Those deep brown beautiful eyes were mesmerizing. "I suppose we could give it a try and see what happens." The words came out so quickly she shocked herself. He wasn't so bad after all, she concluded.

"You won't regret it, I promise you that. We're going to Central Park tomorrow and if it wouldn't interfere with your plans too much I would love for you and Tiffany to join us."

"We don't have any plans set in stone for the week. We figured we would get up everyday and decide what we wanted to do. I'll talk to her and let you know in the morning."

"Great. Wait right here. The limo driver had stopped and opened the door for Ja'Ron. He stepped out and tipped the driver.

Then he came to the other side to let her out. Don't forget your flowers." She smiled as she got out of the limo and entered the hotel.

When they reached the third floor of the hotel Ja'Ron hit the stop button.

"*Uh...uh...*" Her heartbeat sped up. "What are you doing?"

His gaze traveled from her eyes down to her throat as he watched the lump form in her throat. "Something I've wanted to do since the first time I saw you." Without another word he swept her into his arms and kissed her. It was a nice, slow and seductive kiss.

She wanted to stop him but couldn't find the strength too. *He's a great kisser.*

He stopped and looked at her while he traced her cheekbones with his fingertips. "I have never been so drawn to any other woman before."

Hearing his last comment caused her mood to suddenly change and she frowned. She remembered when Robert spoke that same line with her and she had foolishly fallen for it. "Humph... Who do you think you're fooling?"

"I'm not trying to fool anyone. I'm being honest with you."

"A man with your looks and your personality could have any woman he wanted. So please don't try that bull line with me, I'm not falling for it. You men are all alike."

"That's not fair, all men are not alike. You're right, I probably could have any woman I want but I'm not like that at all. Unlike some men, I don't go around hurting or disrespecting women. Words are so powerful so when I say something it's not a front or a line I'm running. It is truly from my heart. So listen up carefully.

At times he's a bit arrogant, but she kind of liked that about him. She gave him her undivided attention. "You are indeed special and I intend to show you just how special you are." Her stomach fluttered as he spoke. She was speechless. She was definitely attracted to him. The question was how would she handle it? She didn't want to be hurt again. He winked at her and grabbed her hand as he started the elevator back up.

They reached the fifth floor and walked toward her room. "Renée, I really enjoyed your company tonight and I know this is just the beginning." He lowered his face so that his lips would meet hers once again. As he kissed her ever so passionately, she knew she wanted more from him. She parted her lips and he gladly allowed his tongue to enter her mouth. Their tongues entangled as he deepened the kiss. She felt her body weaken.

A slight moan escaped her throat. She jerked back. "Sorry I…"

"Shhh…it's okay." He could feel the effect they were both experiencing from each other. He embraced her. "You and I are going places, trust me. You better go on into your room, before I take you to mine. I don't think you're ready for that." She nodded. "I'll talk to you in the morning. Good night sweetheart."

She walked into the room, closed the door and leaned against it. She whispered, "Trust him… will I be able to do that?" She closed her eyes and shook her head. The television was still on. Renée peeked over toward the bed to see if Tiffany was sleeping. "Good, sleeping beauty is knocked out. Lucky for me." She took off her shoes and quietly walked toward her bed, attempting not to wake Tiffany. She turned off the television. As soon as she finished undressing and was into her night gown Tiffany turned her lamp on.

"Hey girlfriend, so how was it?"

She gasped while grabbing her chest. "Geez Tiffany, I thought you were sleeping. Everything was fine."

"Girl, I told you about being so jumpy. Are you ever going to grow out of that?"

Renée rolled her eyes at her friend. "Shut up Tiffany."

"Well what did y'all do?"

Renée gave her all the details. "I did have a nice time and I haven't felt this good in a long time. I'm glad I went out with him."

Tiffany sat up in the bed and her entire face was glowing. "Ok. What now?" She placed a finger up to her mouth and smirked while waiting for an answer.

Renée raised an eyebrow. "What do you mean by that, what now?"

"Are you two going to see more of each other?"

"Maybe."

"Wrong answer, it's either yes or no."

"You're so pushy."

"Give me a straight answer and I won't have to be."

"Yes, I think we will spend more time with each other. Dang girl!"

"Yes! I knew you guys would make a nice couple, I bet you…"

"Hold on, before you get any bright ideas in that cute little head of yours, I didn't say we were getting married or anything. I simply said we were going to spend more time together. No strings attached."

"Oh, you two will be married someday." She threw her hand up to forbid Renée from speaking. "You just remember I told you that." She had a wide grin on her face. "I can't wait to tell Keith."

She shook her head at her friend. "Whatever, Tiffany. Anyways, he wanted to know if I wanted to go to Central Park tomorrow."

Pouting she asked, "Well, what about me?"

"Do I sense a little jealousy?" Renée laughed. "I guess he did invite both of us."

"Yeah, that's what I thought. I hope you told him yes. I can hang out with Marsha and Jeremy if you two would like to hang out alone for a while. It'll be fun."

"How did you know Marsha and Jeremy were going?"

"Girl, he spends quality time with them both. It's not like he just throws Jeremy off on Marsha to care for all the time. He not only appreciates what she does for them, but he shows it. Marsha is like a mom to Ja'Ron since his mom is not physically here anymore. Most of the time when he vacations, they are all on vacation together. He would love it even more if Carla were able to spend more time with them because family is so precious to him. I don't know too many men who would have done what he has done. You know that's asking a lot when you drop a baby off to a single man without an explanation at all."

"Dang girl, I didn't ask you to get all deep on a sista. He seems like a great person. Anyways, I told him I would let him know in the morning if we were going or not."

"Don't wait until morning, call him now and let him know. If you don't, you know I will." Tiffany got up and went into the restroom and Renée dialed his number.

"Hi Renée, I'm glad you called."

She paused and had a puzzled look on her face. "Uh... hi, how did you know it was me?"

"A lucky guess."

"Oh… well I was just calling to let you know that we would be joining you and your family tomorrow."

"Wonderful! I just have one request though."

She raised an eyebrow. "What's the request?"

"Although I have a feeling this won't be a problem for you, but do you think Tiffany can be ready by eleven? We want to make it in time for a particular show at the children's theatre starting at noon." They both laughed knowing it would be a challenge for Tiffany to be ready on time.

"Yeah, I'll drag her out of here by then. Good night Ja'Ron."

"See ya tomorrow, sweet dreams gorgeous."

Tiffany shouted, "Good morning everyone!"

Renée followed behind her, "Good morning Jeremy, Marsha, and Ja'Ron."

All three of them replied together, "Morning ladies."

Ja'Ron said, "I don't believe my girl Tiffany is ten minutes early. This has to be recorded somewhere."

"Watch it Ja'Ron. I'm not late for everything you know." She threw her head up high in the air.

Even Jeremy joined everyone in laughter. Then he said, "Aunt Tiffany, you're so funny."

After arriving at Central Park they all went to the children's theatre to view the play. Jeremy was so excited. Then they took him to the discovery center and Marsha and Tiffany offered to stay with him while he attended a couple of workshops there. Ja'Ron was glad because he wanted to spend some time alone with Renée. They took several tours around the park and she especially admired the beauty of each garden and the lovely waterfalls. She couldn't remember the last time she had so much fun. A few hours later they met back up with Tiffany, Marsha, and Jeremy. They had dinner and then returned to the hotel. They were all worn out from their busy day.

"Daddy, I really like Renée. Is she your girlfriend?"

"Not yet, but daddy is working on it. I'm glad you like her. That means a lot to me. Go on and take your shower so we can get ready for bed."

"Daddy, I had a lot of fun today."

"I'm glad you enjoyed yourself. I love you." He gave him a big hug and sent him into the bathroom. While Jeremy was in the shower Ja'Ron dialed Carla's number. She wasn't home so he left a message.

"Hey Carla, its Ja'Ron. Before I leave New York, I need to talk to you about Jeremy. Since Tiffany and Renée will be joining us for dinner tomorrow, I would like to meet with you earlier in the day. Call me and let me know what time is good for you."

He sighed as he pulled up in front of her condominium. "There's no turning back now," he muttered as he knocked on the door.

"Hey bro, come on in. Do you want something to drink?"

"Naw, I'm cool. I see you've done some redecorating. I like it."

She poured herself a large glass of lemonade. "Yeah, you know me, I'm always changing things. What's going on with Jeremy? Is something wrong?"

"Nothing's wrong with him. I just wanted to see how you would feel about me having legal guardianship over him or adopting him." Her eyes got so huge he thought they were going to pop out of her head. The glass of lemonade slipped from her hands. "What's wrong Carla? You look like you've just seen a ghost."

She stood there hypnotized for a moment. "Uh… uh… I wasn't expecting that to come out of your mouth." She rushed into the kitchen to grab something to clean up the mess she had just made.

"Give me that, let me help you."

"I have it under control, thanks."

"I've had Jeremy since he was a baby and it doesn't seem like you'll ever have the time to spend with him, so I want you to legally give him to me."

Still fidgeting, she shook her head in disbelief and said, "I can't do that."

"Why not Carla? You don't want him to live with you. Or do you?" He sighed. "And why are you fidgeting so?"

"You don't understand. It's not that easy. I have a headache." She got up and began rambling through the cabinet to find a pain reliever.

"What's so hard about it? Talk to me. You don't want him back do you?" She had a strange look on her face and he couldn't figure it out.

"You know I can't take him back with my schedule. I just can't deal with this right now okay. Let me think about it for a while and I'll let you know."

"Ok. I really didn't mean to upset you."

"Ja'Ron, I knew that one day I would have to deal with this but I didn't think it would be this soon."

"I don't want to add more stress to the situation, but I will tell you that if you agree to this we would have to also get the father to agree with it. Can you tell me anything about his father? Do you know where he is?

"Uh...yes. She closed her eyes for a moment. "I know where he is but I am not prepared at this time to tell you anything about him. Please understand that and give me some time to figure out what to do. I'll tell you what, I'll come to Detroit in a few months and we'll talk more about it. Is that okay?"

"I guess it will have to be. However, I don't want this to be on hold for a long time."

She began to relax a little, and took advantage of the moment to gracefully change the conversation. "So what's up with Ms. Renée?"

"What do you mean by that?"

"You know what I mean. I haven't heard you even mention any woman since you've had Jeremy, and I know you're attracted to her. I detected it in your voice the very first time you mentioned her. Then when I met her after the show, I noticed the twinkle in your eyes."

"Oh stop it." He smiled. "I guess you're right. I intend to spend a lot of time with her and you never know..."

"I never know what?" Both of her eyebrows shot up. "You couldn't be considering getting married. Are you?"

"I'm not getting any younger and I don't want to spend all my life without that special woman to share it with. So yeah, I'm ready to find that special woman to marry and have children with, and I think Renée just might be her."

"So I guess you have finally gotten over Destiny's trifling behind. Although she's my friend, I'm glad you didn't marry her."

"If I had married Destiny I would have been so miserable and yes we would have been divorced by now. She never really loved me; she just wanted what I could offer her. It was all about her and she didn't want to contribute anything at all to our relationship. Do you still talk to her? Where is she now?"

"She's living in California now and we don't talk as much as we used to. I did a show there a few months ago so I did spend a few days with her. Well I'm glad that you have found someone. I hope that she is the one for you."

"Me too. I better go now. He headed toward the door. I'll see you later for dinner okay. I love you."

"I love you too. Bye."

SEVEN

"Ooh… that felt good," Renée muttered as she stretched on final time before rising from her bed. She opened her blinds to let some sunshine into her room. "It is absolutely gorgeous outside. What a great way to start off the work week." She felt energized and ready to tackle her day-to-day business again. The week in New York turned out to be better than planned. She enjoyed the time she spent with Ja'Ron and his family, but she still had to be cautious. After showering, she had a tough decision to make… like what to wear today? After going through the suit section in her closet three times, she decided to wear a cream colored suit.

Renée checked her appointment book to see what she had lined up for the week. "Oh my, the closing on the hall is scheduled for this morning. Why did I think it was later today? I need to call Jessica to let her know that I will be late." She glanced at the clock. "Dang, I better get going. I'll call Jessica from my car," she said as she grabbed her briefcase and headed out the door.

"Good morning Renée Bridal's, Jessica speaking. How may I help you?"

"Good morning Jessica. How's everything?"

"Hi Renée, everything's fine. How was your trip? I just knew for sure that I would hear from you sooner than today."

Renée chuckled. "My trip was wonderful, thanks for asking. I know it's hard to believe that I didn't check in, but I wanted you to know that I fully trusted you."

Jessica smiled. "Thanks Renée, I really appreciate the trust and confidence that you have in me. Before I forget, you had a phone call this morning but he didn't want to leave a message. He said he would try and reach you later."

"Hmm… I wonder who that could have been. Oh well, if its important he'll call back. Anyway, I was calling to let you know that I have a meeting this morning, so I'll be a little late. I'm sure you can handle things until I get there."

"No problem. I'll see you when you get here."

"Jessica, I almost forgot, I need you to call Tiffany and let her know that we need to begin working on the Bostic's wedding today. See if she can come in at three thirty. See ya later and thanks again."

She began to think about how good she felt being able to leave work for a change and not worry about things getting all screwed up. *Jessica has been a blessing to the shop. She has definitely proved herself responsible. I'm just glad that I can finally trust someone other than Tiffany to handle the business while I'm away.*

She parked the car and walked into the realtor's office. She was more than ready to sign on the dotted line. She was very pleased at how smooth the meeting had gone. Afterward she headed straight to work. She chatted with Jessica for a few minutes and gave her the bracelet and a pair of earrings she had purchased for her from New York.

"Thanks Renée. I love them."

"You're welcome. Well Jessica, I think I better get to work now."

"All of your written messages are on your desk."

"Thanks." Renée proceeded to go to her office. She unlocked the door and…

"Oh my God! What on earth?" She threw one hand over her mouth. "Who sent these beautiful roses?" There were bouquets of red, yellow, and white roses all over the room. "Did I forget it was my birthday or something?" She was stunned. She sat her briefcase down at the door and walked over toward her desk. She noticed a card attached to one of the bouquets on her desk. It read:

Welcome back gorgeous. Our time together in New York was wonderful. I would love for you to join me for dinner tonight. I hope six or seven will be fine. I'll call you soon to confirm our date and the time. I hope you have a great day!"
                        Ja'Ron Moss

She smiled as she glanced around the room again. She then walked back to her office door to retrieve her briefcase. Jessica walked into the room.

"Renée, what a wonderful surprise, huh?"

"Yes, this was a surprise indeed."

"My goodness, you're glowing. Are you going to tell me about him?"

She brought her hand up to her face. "Am I really glowing?" She felt a little embarrassed.

"Oh yes, that's a true glow you have. Well do I have to wait to hear about him?"

"It's just a guy I met at Tiffany's party. Actually he's a good friend of Keith and Tiffany's. While I was in New York I ran into him again. We went out and…"

As Jessica's eyes lit up, her mouth dropped. She was too excited. "And what Renée?"

She smirked. "Umm… we'll see what happens."

Jessica hugged Renée. "I'm so happy for you. From the look of this room, I'll say someone is in love. I gotta get back to work."

She decided not to comment on the love statement. "Getting back to work sounds like a good idea Jessica. Did you reach Tiffany?"

"Yes, she said three thirty is not a problem and she'll be here on time."

She rolled her eyes. "Yeah, I bet she will."

Renée was busy going through some paperwork when her phone rang.

"Yes."

"Renée, Mr. Moss is on line four."

"Thanks Jessica."

"Hi, Ja'Ron. How are you?"

"I'm doing very well."

"Thank you so much for the flowers. They are beautiful."

"You're welcome. They remind me of you. So are you available for dinner tonight?"

"Yes, and seven will work best for me."

"Alright, seven it shall be. I know you're busy but I need to get your address and home phone number." She gave him her address and they exchanged phone numbers.

The time was passing by quickly; before she knew anything it was three fifteen. "Tiffany should be here in a half hour." She got up to get something to drink. She stood and looked out the window and reflected back on the dinner date she had in New York with Ja'Ron. She was deep in thought when…

"You go girl! Who bought out the rose garden?"

She jumped. "Tiffany, do you ever knock? I wasn't expecting you so soon."

She tilted her head. "Why should I knock when there's no one in here but you?" She smirked. "Huh?"

"It's called courtesy. Try it sometime."

"Awe girl, you're just touchy because I interrupted your deep thoughts. I bet I can easily guess whom you were thinking about too." She brought a rose up to her nose. "Hmm… I love the smell of roses, so who did they come from?" Before Renée could answer her Tiffany was already on a mystery hunt. She found the card and began to read it. "I knew it! Ja'Ron knows how to work it doesn't he?" Renée shook her head. Tiffany slapped her hands together and sat down. "Well let's get down to business so you can get out of here and prepare for your date."

"Tiffany, you're too much. How are you feeling?"

"I feel fine. I think I'm over the morning sickness. I have an appointment later this week."

"Good." She handed a copy of the Bostic's file to Tiffany.

They began going over the Bostic's wedding plans. "Renée this is a big account, huh?"

"Yes. We'll make a lot of money on this one. The bride is only twenty-one. Her brother came in with her and said, give her whatever she wants. Just send me the bill."

"That's what I'm talking about. Spoiled rotten, huh? So is the deal completed for the hall?"

"Yes. I wish you had come to the meeting earlier. The place is now ours." Although the money invested was her own, she still liked for her friend to be included on all aspects of the business transactions. That way if something ever happened to her, Tiffany could step in and take over with no problem.

"There was no reason for me to be there, I knew you had everything under control. Besides, I knew you would fill me in on the details. The hiring is completed."

"What about Fonso? Did he decide to take the chef position?"

"Yes, he did."

"That's wonderful." She sighed. "The building is in excellent condition. All we need to do is redecorate it to our taste. Everything will be ready and in place for the grand opening." The two women did a dance around the office.

Tiffany looked up at the clock. "Renée, its almost five thirty. You have to go and get ready for your date. If Jessica's already gone I'll lock everything up.

"Alright, as soon as I gather a few things I'm outta here."

Ja'Ron was ready for his date. He went into Jeremy's room to check on him before he left. Jeremy was busy playing a video game.

"Hey buddy. I'm getting ready to leave now. You can read a story to Marsha tonight okay."

Without taking his eyes off his game he said, "Ok, dad. Dad, are you going out with Ms. Renée tonight?"

"Yes. Are you okay with that?"

"Yeah, I think she's cool."

Ja'Ron turned to leave the room and all of a sudden something caught his attention. He turned back toward his preoccupied son. "Jeremy, is that a new game?"

"Yep."

He looked curiously at Jeremy as he continued to play the game. "I don't recall buying that one for you. Did Marsha get that for you?"

"Nope."

"If I didn't buy it and neither did Marsha, where did you get it from?"

"I got it when we were in New York."

"Oh, okay. Carla got it for you."

"No, some lady named Destiny. Aunt Carla said she's her friend."

Ja'Ron looked puzzled. "Ok squirt. Don't play the game too long and I want you in bed on time."

"Ok, dad. Bye. I hope you have fun."

"Bye dad, I hope you have fun," Ja'Ron mimicked. "What's up with this? No hug!"

Jeremy paused the game to give his dad a hug and then he went right back to playing his new game. Ja'Ron pulled his door up a little and proceeded to go downstairs. "Marsha, I'm getting ready to leave."

"Alright Ja'Ron. Hey, I'm glad to see you finally dating. From the short time we spent with her I think she's a very nice young lady. I hope you have a good time."

"Thanks. I'm sure I will. By the way Marsha, Jeremy has a new video game that he's upstairs playing. He said he got it from one of Carla's friends. Do you know anything about that?"

"Yeah, I think her name was Destiny. I think she's a model and she works with Carla sometimes." His look was perplexed. "Is everything alright Ja'Ron?"

"Yes. I was just a little surprised that no one mentioned this to me."

"To be honest, I didn't think anything of it. Do you know Destiny?"

"Yes, I use to date her. Actually I almost married her."

Marsha's mouth dropped. "What! I've never heard you talk about her before now." Marsha was very concerned. "Oh boy, are you still hung up on her?"

"Not at all. I was just wondering why Carla didn't mention that she was in New York. I guess it really doesn't matter." For some reason he felt a little strange finding this out. He would have to ask Carla about it the next time they talked. "Oh well, I better get out of here before I'm late for my date."

"Have a great time."

He kissed her cheek. "Thanks. I intend to."

"I wonder who this could be calling." She laid her lipstick case on the bathroom counter. "Hello."

"Hi, Renée. Are you ready yet?"

"Didn't I just leave you? What do you want?" She laughed.

"Girl, you know I had to call and check up on you before you went out."

"I'm fine Tiffany. I was just putting on my lipstick when you called." The doorbell rang. "Gotta go, someone's at the door."

"Have fun, bye."

"Hello Ja'Ron. Come on in. You're early. Would you like something to drink?"

He chuckled as he stepped inside. "No thanks. These are for you."

She took the bouquet of flowers. "Thank you, they're beautiful. I'll find a vase for them. Come in and have a seat."

He followed her into the living room. The room was carpeted winter white, complimented by burgundy and white Italian style furniture. The wall was graced by a beautiful portrait of her and was surrounded by other African-American paintings. He wanted to see more of the house. When she returned to the room he said, "Renée, I think I would like something to drink."

"Ok, just follow me into the kitchen." As they walked past the family room, he stopped to peek through the glass doors. She stopped, "Go ahead and check it out." She smirked at his interest to see how she lived as he opened the door. This room was carpeted in purple and there was a fireplace in the middle of the room. Over the fireplace hung a nice portrait of Tiffany and Renée. The purple leather furniture was gorgeous. The purple and gold silk flower arrangement in the room added a finishing touch.

"You have excellent taste Renée."

"Thank you, I'm glad you like it. Let's get you something to drink so that we can go soon."

"I'm right behind you," he said smiling.

The restaurant was very crowded. "Ja'Ron please excuse me for a moment."

"No problem, just tell me what you want to drink and I'll place the order while you're gone."

"Ice tea is fine with me, thanks." As she entered the restroom, she thought she saw a familiar face. "Naw it couldn't be," she said as she shrugged her shoulders. After putting on a fresh coat of lipstick she returned to her table.

"So, Ja'Ron…"

"Hello Renée." The voice was deep and recognizable. She suddenly felt a cold chill run down her spine. She slowly turned around to see who had called her. She swallowed hard and ran her fingers through her hair. Ja'Ron immediately noticed her discomfort.

"Yes." She forced a smile. *I don't believe this and what was he doing back in town,* she wondered.

"I saw you walk in and I just wanted to come over and speak. I just moved back a few months ago."

A little voice cried out, "Daddy." He pulled the little boy closer to his side.

Oh God, it's the child. That must have been her I saw a few minutes ago. She was trying hard to keep her composure. "That's too kind of you." She glared at him. Ja'Ron sat there curiously and patiently waiting to find out who this man was.

"How have you been? I heard your business is doing very well. I'm happy for you." Ja'Ron continued to observe them in silence. He gathered that this was the man who had broken her heart.

Yeah, I bet you are, she thought but didn't say anything to him. He looked over at Ja'Ron.

"Are you going to introduce me to the lucky man?"

She felt her eye twitch as she gave him an annoying look. She sighed as she turned toward Ja'Ron. "Ja'Ron Moss this is Robert Colby. Robert is my ex-husband."

As they shook hands Robert said, "You look familiar. Are you the owner of the clothing boutique that just opened here in Ann Arbor?"

"Yes I am," replied Ja'Ron.

"A very impressive boutique. Excellent quality, you should do well in the area. It's so nice to meet you." Renée just wanted him to leave. "Well, I won't interrupt your evening any longer. I just came over to say hello." He turned back toward Renée. "It's nice to see you again and as always you look beautiful. Have a pleasant evening." He grabbed the child's hand and walked away.

She shook her head as she twirled one of her long curls.

"Are you okay?" Ja'Ron asked. "If you want to leave we can dine somewhere else."

"No, I'm fine. I'm not going to let him ruin my evening."

"Would you like to talk about it?"

"There's not much to talk about, but if you want to know what happened I'll tell you." She added a little sugar and then took a drink of her ice tea. "I was once happily married to Robert. He slept with my cousin and now they have a child together. I guess she was able to give him something that I couldn't give him."

Ja'Ron wanted to have children but if she was unable to conceive there were other options. One thing for sure, he knew he was not willing to let her go because of it. "Are you saying that you cannot have children?"

"No, I'm not saying that at all. After we had been married for a few years, we began to focus on starting a family. We were very happy when I found out I was pregnant. Well, that all ended after I lost my baby. I did nothing wrong, but he blamed me for it and stop communicating with me. My cousin Mya was living with us for a while so I suppose she consoled him. One day Tiffany and I decided to go out of town and when we returned unexpectedly, we found them in my house, in my bed together. Furthermore, as you can see, she was able to give him a son. End of story." Her expression was very cold.

"Wow, how could someone be so cruel? No one deserves that at all." The waiter came to take their order.

"It was truly the best thing for me. My business would not have been as successful if I remained in that marriage."

He decided to be very bold since they were on the subject of marriage. "So would you ever like to be married again someday?" She glanced away from him for a moment. He thought, *Oh boy, you shouldn't have asked that question just yet. You have pushed your luck a little too far.*

"You know, if I were asked that a year or so ago my answer would have been absolutely not. But deep down inside I know that I would like to be married someday and have children. I have a great business and I think that my life would be more complete then. But the next time it will last, so I'll have to be very careful who I decide to settle down with."

He felt so relieved at her answer. "So where do we go from here?"

She raised an eyebrow. "Meaning?"

"I want us to develop a more serious relationship." The waiter appeared with their food. She didn't respond, instead she picked up her fork and began eating. He chuckled. *She's not making this easy.* "Renée, why are you ignoring me? What are you afraid of?

"Afraid – I'm not afraid of anything." She was definitely lying to herself.

"Good, then please allow me to repeat the question. So where do we go from here?"

"Look you're a nice man, but…"

"But what? You're afraid that I might hurt you. Aren't you?"

Her body stiffened from what he just asked. "I have to protect myself."

"Everyone is not like your ex-husband. You can't let him control your life and that's exactly what you have been doing. I bet you haven't dated since your divorce, have you?"

"As a matter of fact I haven't. So what's it to you?"

"Don't get defensive. I'm just trying to make a point. You have to move on and enjoy the fullness of life, that's what I have decided to do now myself. You know what?"

"What?"

"Believe it or not, I've been hurt and disappointed myself."

She gave him a *yeah-right* look. "Please elaborate."

"I was in a serious relationship once. We were engaged, but then we both realized that marriage for us would have been a big mistake, so we broke off the engagement. I loved her but she was very selfish and was not willing to change. Everything was all about what I could do for her. I dated occasionally afterward, but when Jeremy came to live with me, all my free time was spent with him. I decided after seven years, I needed to make some changes in my life. Just like yourself, I worked hard to build my business, but now that I am comfortable with what I have it's time for me to fulfill the rest of my life." He paused to gulp down some water.

"I care about you a lot and I want you to be my woman." Ja'Ron studied her every move.

She wanted him to be her man, but could she trust him. She knew she needed to open her heart again if she would ever settle down with anyone. Her attraction to him grew stronger and stronger each time she spoke with him or saw him.

"Renée."

"Yes Ja'Ron, you're right and I would like to develop a more serious relationship with you also." She couldn't believe how quickly she spoke the words that had just come tumbling out of her mouth. However it was the truth, she decided. She unconsciously licked her suddenly dry lips. They both smiled.

"Whew, I was hoping that you would give us a chance. I promise, you won't regret it. Let's get out of here." He paid the bill and they went back to her place.

"Would you like to come in?" she asked.

"Sure."

"You can pull your car into the garage."

She unlocked the door and he closed the door behind them.

"Why don't you make yourself comfortable in the family room. You do remember where it is don't you?" She smirked. "I'm going to change into something more comfortable."

She returned to the room dressed in a sweat suit. He had put on some jazz. "Would you like something to drink?"

"No thanks. What I would like right now is to dance with you." She walked into his waiting arms. They danced all over the room. He pulled her closer to him and she could feel every muscle in his body. They stared at each other as he brought one hand up to caress her face. She swallowed hard. He ran his fingers through her hair. "You are beautiful." Their breathing intensified as his tongue brushed against her lower lip. He pulled her even closer as he parted her mouth with his tongue for a full entrance. She melted as their mouths mated, sensuously, and deep. A low moan escaped her throat. His hands roamed all over her body when…

"Ding-dong." Renée jerked back. She looked over at the clock. "Who could that be at this hour? I'll be right back." She looked through the peephole to see who was ringing the doorbell. She started laughing as she opened the door. "Girl, you always have bad timing."

"I was out in the area and thought I would stop by. So how was your date?"

She knew Tiffany was just being nosy. "Ja'Ron, Tiffany's here she wanted to know how the date went."

"Oh that's mean! I didn't know he was here." Ja'Ron came out of the family room smiling.

"Dang Ja'Ron you're looking happy, whassup!"

"Girl, you are a trip," Ja'Ron said as he hugged her.

"Whoa, you're a little plump there aren't you?" He rubbed her belly.

She hit Ja'Ron on his shoulder. "Shut up, it'll be gone in a few months." They all laughed. "Well, I guess I better go. I was just out cruising and thought I would stop by. Have a good night you two." She giggled as she closed the door behind her.

"You two are totally different aren't you?"

"Yeah, I guess that's why we get along so well. I wouldn't trade in our friendship for anything in the world."

"Well sweetheart, it's getting late and I want you to get your beauty rest. I'll talk to you tomorrow." He gave her a quick peck on the cheek and left.

EIGHT

Carla watched Destiny as she strutted through the doors of the restaurant they were dining in. She stopped to talk to a couple of men she knew before reaching their table. "Hi Carla, what's going on girlfriend?"

"Hi Destiny." She stood up to embrace her. "Have you been working pretty steady?"

"Yeah, work has been great. I have been offered a couple of jobs outside of the country, but I haven't decided yet if I'm going to accept either one of them. I also got an offer to do a show in Detroit for some charity event."

"Oh, it may be the same one that I'm doing. It'll be cool if it was the same one since we haven't worked together in a while. Are you going to accept it?" The waitress appeared to take their orders.

"Girl, I don't know yet. So how's your brother and Jeremy doing?"

"They're doing fine. As a matter of fact I'll be visiting them soon." The waitress returned with their drinks. Destiny took a sip of her diet coke.

"Jeremy is growing up fast and he's a nice looking kid. It was good to see him while they were in New York."

"Yeah, Ja'Ron has taken very good care of him. Which brings up why I needed to talk with you."

"Whassup?"

"While Ja'Ron was in New York he asked me about either adopting Jeremy or obtaining legal guardianship over him."

Destiny tilted her head slightly. "I think that's great. What did you tell him?"

"You know I panicked, but he agreed to give me a little time to think it over."

Destiny had a devilish grin on her face. "Is Ja'Ron still as fine as he use to be? What is he doing these days?"

"You know he will always look good...it's in the genes. He opened another boutique up in Ann Arbor not too long ago. He's doing great."

"So, is there a special lady in his life yet?" She lit a cigarette. "Curious, that's all." Truth being, she felt mischievous.

Carla watched her for a moment to detect any devilish expressions that may be present. Figuring the coast was clear she said, "As a matter of fact, there is a young lady that has his head spinning right now." She smiled.

"Oh yeah," she said after asking the waitress for a refill. "You like her?"

"Yeah, she seems like a cool lady, she's very successful."

"What does she do?"

"She owns a bridal shop, and an entertainment hall."

Destiny didn't like that at all. She was feeling jealous. "Head spinning, huh? Maybe I'll go back to Detroit to stir up some things."

Carla was losing her touch because she had misread Destiny. She knew how devious she could be. "I wouldn't do that if I were you. You know you can care less about Ja'Ron. If you don't want to get hurt I suggest you stay away from them."

Destiny finished her drink. She wiped the corners of her mouth and pasted a devilish grin on her face. "Oh come on, it'll be so much fun. He's such a wonderful guy and besides I do still care about him. You never know maybe he and I can work things out." she laughed, while giving the waitress her credit card.

"Destiny, promise me you won't go trying to interfere," Carla said pointing her finger. She knew Destiny too well and she knew Ja'Ron wouldn't tolerate any foolishness coming from her.

"Ok. I promise." *I think I will do the show in Detroit after all. It's been a long time since I've been there.* She knew there was no way Ja'Ron would take her back, but she didn't want him to be happy with anyone else either. Everything was cool before knowing he hadn't settled down yet but now…

Carla checked her watch. "Destiny I hate to cut this visit short, but I have to get ready for the show tonight. This conversation will have to be continued at a later date."

"Look Carla, don't sweat it. I think you should go ahead and give Jeremy to Ja'Ron. That'll probably be best for everyone." She smirked because she had something else in mind.

Carla looked at her and boy was she puzzled. "That's it. You don't have anything else to say."

She shook her head while filing a nail. "Nope."

"Ok sweetie, thanks. I really have to be going. I'll be in touch. Bye." Carla gave her a kiss on the cheek before leaving her.

She muttered, "Carla my friend, I won't lose this time. If Ja'Ron doesn't want to be with me, he's not going to be happy with anyone else. I'll make sure of that."

"You're the man, I hear Mr. Moss," Keith said as he entered Ja'Ron's office.

"You think so?"

"Oh yeah, from what I have heard you are winning Renée over big time. I think you two deserve each other and I'm happy for you."

"Yeah, I'm happier. I was worried that she wouldn't give me a chance in the beginning, but she finally came around."

"What does Marsha and Jeremy think of her?"

"Oh they absolutely adore her. Jeremy has really gotten attached to her.

"That's great. So, did you hear anything from Carla yet?"

"No. I think she's trying to avoid me. I've called and left several messages. She hasn't returned my calls though. I'm beginning to wonder if she's trying to hide something. Her behavior in New York was very strange." He rubbed his goatee.

"Hmm… To me it seems like she's trying to buy herself some time for some reason or another."

"I definitely think that you're right about that. I don't want to pressure her to much but I was hoping to get this settled soon, so that I can move on to my next agenda."

"Which is?"

"Renee." He grinned. "No need to expand on that."

"I gotcha brother."

Everything was in place for the grand opening of Majestic Hall. Invitations had been sent out and RSVP's have been received. They were expecting over four hundred people to attend tonight. "Is Ja'Ron coming for the grand opening?" Tiffany asked.

"Why of course. Carla is supposed to come also." She touched Tiffany's belly. "You're really beginning to show now."

"I know and the baby is very active. The ultrasound is scheduled for next week."

"Activeness is a good sign. Are you going to find out what you're having?"

"No, we decided that we wanted to be surprised."

"I hope that one day, I'll have a child. You know I'm not getting any younger."

Tiffany gulped down some juice. "You will. I'm going to get ready to leave now so that I can be well rested for tonight."

"Alright, I'll be leaving here shortly myself."

"Goodness, this place is beautiful," Destiny said as she pulled up in the parking lot. There were waterfalls in selected spots before reaching the entrance. She took in every detail as she proceeded to the entrance. "This place looks like a palace from the outside." There was also security on the premises. On each side of the entrance on the lawn, stood lighted figures of two horses pulling a carriage. "I can't wait to see the inside." She was in awe as she toured the building. "I have never seen something so beautiful before." From the chandeliers down to the carpet Destiny knew this woman was very tasteful in everything she does. She muttered, "she must have spent a fortune decorating this place. Ja'Ron likes a classy lady. I can't wait to see what she looks like."

As Renée got out of her car, she could here the band playing nice, soft music. Dinner was to be served promptly at seven o'clock. Renée went directly into the kitchen to make sure everything was okay. The chef and his staff were one of the best around town. She was grateful Fonso had taken the job. She knew the guest tonight would be very pleased. Meanwhile, Tiffany was checking in with the head hostess, Shantell.

"Hi Shantell, how are things going?"

"Hi Tiffany. Everything is running smooth."

"No problems with the guest list."

"No. Actually there was only one lady who showed up but wasn't on the list. Very gorgeous, she looked like a model. She said she was surprised that she was not listed."

"What was her name? Did she give you a hard time?"

"Destiny was her name and she didn't give me a hard time at all. I told her she wasn't on the list. She thanked me for double checking and without another word she left." Shantell was relieved because she hated drama. "I spoke with your husband earlier."

"Oh yeah."

"He's so down to earth. I like that." Renée joined them and greeted Shantell. Shantell spoke to Renée and then continued her conversation with Tiffany. "Please tell me, who was that fine hunk he walked in with?" She shook her head and lifted her hand. "That man would make any woman go weak in the knees. Fine, fine, fine." Renée was amused as she listened and watched Shantell drooled. Tiffany tapped Renée before speaking.

"Girl, that's Ja'Ron Moss." She glanced at Renée. "He's off limits, so all you can do is look and drool over him.

Shantell sighed. "Dang, I always lose out." All three of the women laughed.

"Well, whoever the lucky woman is, she better know that if she screws up, there are plenty of us who would jump at a chance to be with him. He most certainly had a lot of heads turning tonight." Renée smirked and shook her head.

Tiffany said, "Well Shantell it was nice chatting with you, but we have to go now. It's almost time for our introductions."

"Alright boss. By the way, Jessica is doing a great job tonight. See ya later."

The evening was filled with entertainment. It began with a fashion show, singing, and comedy. Back stage Renée and Tiffany peaked out into the crowd. Renée spotted Ja'Ron and Keith right away. She was glad to see Carla sitting at the table also. She wasn't sure if she would definitely make it but she assured Renée that she would try. Everyone appeared to be enjoying themselves and everything was running right on schedule.

Jessica was the emcee for the evening. She announced, "Now let me introduce you to the owners of Majestic's Hall Ms. Renée Colby and Mrs. Tiffany Russell."

The entire guest stood to their feet and there was an alarming round of applause as Renée and Tiffany walked across the stage. Keith and Ja'Ron stood there smiling as they watched their lovely women beam with joy. They both looked beautiful in their sequin gowns.

Renée began:

"Good evening ladies and gentlemen. First of all I would like to thank you all for making the grand opening of Majestic's Hall a memorable night for both Tiffany and I. This is truly a dream that has come true for me and I thank our heavenly father for making it possible." Applause. "I also want to thank my mother who is no longer with me for encouraging me to pursue all of my dreams. I know if she were here today, she would be very proud of my accomplishments. I want to also thank my friends for all the support and advice they have given me. Again, thank you all for coming. Brace yourself for a shift change as I turn the microphone over to my partner Tiffany Russell." Applause.

Tiffany began:

"I'm going to get a little ghetto on y'all cause I'm feeling good tonight. Those that know me will understand, y'all who don't will eventually understand." She shouted out "Whassup everybody, we did it!" The guest responded in another applause and a loud cheer,"Yeah!" Once the applause simmered down she continued, "Well I think Renée just about summed it all up. But in addition to what she said, I just want to personally thank my beautiful husband Keith Russell for being so supportive in everything that I do. Stand up baby." Keith stood up and offered a slight wave. "Isn't he fine y'all?" she asked as she blew him a kiss.

"Yes he is," the women replied.

Tiffany threw her hands up in the air. "Alright, that's enough. I don't want any of y'all to forget, he belongs to me." The room broke off into laughter. Renee just shook her head at her friend. "Seriously though, I really appreciate everyone who came out tonight to show your support and to wish us well. I also appreciate those who came out to hate, you know the saying, 'don't hate...graduate'." The room laughed and applauded once again. "Please feel free to tour the entire building and remember if you want a classy event, Majestic's is the place to be. Enjoy your evening and God bless you all."

Destiny had managed to slip past the head hostess and she sat in a vacant chair at one of the tables in the back. She had gotten a glimpse of Ja'Ron earlier. *Carla was right - her brother is still fine.* Now she knew who Renée Colby was. She muttered, "She's pretty and very successful. I will not make it easy for her to be with Ja'Ron and that's a promise. Watch out Renée, Destiny's in town." She smirked. "How much do you really care about him?" She stayed for a little while after Renée and Tiffany had given their speeches. She checked her watch and realized she had to get out of there. She didn't want to take a chance on being noticed by Carla or Ja'Ron. From her observance of the lovely couple tonight she knew she had to organize and put her destructive plan into action real soon. "Ja'Ron will belong to me," she proclaimed while speeding from the parking lot.

NINE

The night had finally ended. Renée felt good about the huge turnout, but she was even happier that it was over. All of the guest were gone except for Ja'Ron and Carla who were waiting for her in the ballroom. Tiffany and Keith had just left. Renée had assured Tiffany that she would allow the people hired to lock up do their job. She was more than ready to jump into bed herself. She pulled off her high heels as she walked into the almost vacated room. She looked around and sighed. Suddenly sadness fell upon her as she looked up toward the ceiling. She whispered, "Mom, I wish you were here. I hope I've made you very proud."

"What a night! How are you feeling?" Ja'Ron asked while placing an arm around her waist.

She yawned. "Tired and ready to sink deeply into my bed." She glanced over his shoulder. "Where's Carla?"

"I think she might have gone to the restroom."

"Oh. I hope she enjoyed herself tonight."

"I think she did. Hey, why the sad look?" He tilted her chin upward.

"I was just thinking about my mother. Wishing she was here."

"Trust me baby, she's looking down smiling at her baby girl right now. I know you have made her proud." Her eyes lit up as she smiled at him. He stroked her cheek as he pulled her closer to him, "Renée." He closed his eyes as he held her firmly against him. Hot desire rushed through every inch of his body. He wished he could have her at his house, in his bed tonight. As he held her, he suddenly realized that she was the only woman that he had even considered sharing his home with. He had purchased the home three months before Jeremy came to live with him. He wanted to be careful whom he exposed Jeremy to and he felt very comfortable with her. The few women he casually associated with since Jeremy moved in with him resented not being able to come to his home. He had made it clear to them from the beginning the reason but they didn't believe that he would actually keep his word. When it came to women, he would only bring that special person he wanted to settle down with to his home. He gently ran his hands up and down her back. She felt good in his arms. He was deep in thought when…

"Hey Girl!" Carla shouted. The warm embrace was quickly broken. Carla smiled at him knowing she had interrupted their moment. "I guess you almost forgot I was here, huh Ja'Ron?" She chuckled and elbowed him in the side before turning her focus back on Renée. She pasted a wide grin on her face.

"Congratulations goes out to you and Tiffany on your huge success. What a magnificent grand opening! The hall is absolutely beautiful and everything was so organized. I like your style girl. You and I will get along fine. Whenever I do decide to get married, you and Tiffany are definitely hired."

Renée smiled showing those beautiful white teeth of hers. That was the effect they intended to have on anyone who booked or attended any event at Majestic's. "Thank you so much, Carla. I want you to know that I'm really glad that you were able to make it. I know your schedule is hectic. Your presence truly means a lot to me."

"You're right. My schedule is horrid right now, but I wouldn't have missed this for anything. Not only did my coming mean a lot to you, but it meant a lot to my brother also." She patted Ja'Ron on the shoulder.

"Hmm…" Renée replied. She wondered why it meant so much to Ja'Ron, but decided not to comment on it. "Are you staying for a few days?"

Carla glanced over at Ja'Ron before speaking. She hadn't even told him her length of stay. "I have to fly back out in the morning. I have a photo shoot scheduled for later in the evening." Ja'Ron looked surprised. He was hoping to further discuss Jeremy's custody.

"Oh, that's too bad. I wanted to have you over for dinner and I was hoping to show you the boutique before you left. Maybe next time, huh?" Renée was a little disappointed.

"I'll be back in a few weeks. We can hook up and hang out then. I'm planning to stay for a week or so." Ja'Ron was happy to hear that. He guessed he could wait until then to bring up the subject of Jeremy again.

"I'm going to hold you to that." Renée really liked Carla.

Ja'Ron cleared his throat. "I know that you're tired Renée so we better get ready to go. Would you like to leave your car here and I'll drive you home?"

"Thanks, but I'll be fine. You go ahead and get Carla home so that she can get some rest before her flight leaves in a few hours." She retrieved her shoes and put them back on. "Carla, Jeremy is going to be crushed that he didn't get to spend any time with you."

"I know, but I'll make it up to him. Auntie always does." Renée said good night to security and they all exited the building together. Carla gave her a hug. "Good night Renée."

"Good night Carla, have a safe flight."

"Thanks, I'll see you soon." Carla went to Ja'Ron's car. She was happy for her brother. He and Renée were a perfect match.

Ja'Ron walked Renée to her car. He opened the door and before she could enter the car he swept her into his arms and covered her mouth with his. She melted in his arms as his hands settled right above her tiny waist. She didn't know how much longer she could endure the sensuous kisses they shared without ripping his clothes off of him. She wanted to make love to him, but she wanted the time to be right. She was falling in love with him. "Mmmm…" escaped his throat.

Renée whispered, "You've got to get your sister home."

"Yes, you are right. Call me as soon as you get in."

"Ok Ja'Ron."

When Ja'Ron got into his car, Jazz was playing. Carla was reclined in the passenger seat with her eyes closed. He knew she was tired, so he let her sleep. After fifteen minutes of riding, she awakened. "Ja'Ron. How long was I sleep?"

"Not too long."

"You and Renée look good together. How's it going with you two?"

"I'd say we're doing pretty good," he answered with a smile. He paused for a moment. "I'm in love with her."

Carla patted his leg. " I figured that. Only a fool in your presence would think otherwise."

"I'm going to start looking at rings." He glanced over at her and waited for her response.

Carla raised an eyebrow. "Get outta here!" She searched his face to see if he was just joking. "You're serious, aren't you?"

"Yes I am. I love her, Jeremy loves her, and once you really get to know her you'll love her too. She's everything I need and then some. I'm going to ask her to marry me real soon. How would you feel about that? Not that it matters," he said laughing.

She punched him in his arm. "I think that's great. I'm happy for you."

"I wonder why she hasn't called yet. I hope she made it home okay. I'll give her a few more minutes, and then I'm calling her. I'm going to invite her over to the house soon."

"I'm sure she's okay. She probably wanted to take a shower and get relaxed first. Getting back to what you said a few moments ago, are you telling me that she hasn't been to your house yet?"

"Nope," she hasn't.

"What are you waiting for?" She was shocked.

"Why are you so surprise? You know I don't have women chilling at the house."

"Boy, I thought you were joking when you first told me about your rule on women coming to the crib. I should of known, Mr. Serious. Well I guess she is special." She chuckled. "Whose calling your cell phone this late?"

"I hope its Renée. Hello."

"Hi Ja'Ron. Sorry it took me so long to call, but I wanted to get in the shower first."

He smiled. "That's what Carla just said, I was beginning to worry. I'm glad you made it in safely. We're pulling into the driveway now. Hey, before you hang up I was wondering if you would like to come out to my place on Sunday." Carla shot him a *devilish look*. He pretended not to see her.

Renée had begun to wonder why he hadn't invited her there before now. "Sure. I was planning to go to church, but I can come over afterward. I can get the directions from you later."

"No need. What time do you normally get out of church?"

"Usually by one, why?"

"I'll come and get you."

"You don't have to do that. I can drive there."

"Shhh… I insist. I'll see you around two."

"Ok. Good night." Renée smiled as she hung up the phone. *Could he be the man of her dreams?* she wondered.

"Dang Ja'Ron you don't play around do you?" Carla asked as Ja'Ron unlocked the door.

They stepped inside and he removed his shoes. "Girl, what are you talking about?"

"You're inviting her over Sunday."

"Yeah, is something wrong with that?"

She shook her head. "Not at all, bro." She yawned, while stretching out her arms. "I'm tired. I'm going to shower and then straight to bed myself. Good night Ja'Ron." She kissed his cheek.

"Good night Carla."

TEN

Destiny was suddenly awakened from her dream. She glanced over at the clock. "The alarm didn't go off." It was five thirty in the morning. "I should have asked for a wake up call. Man, I better not miss my flight. I hate rushing around, even if it is my fault." Destiny got up; washed her face, brushed her teeth, and quickly got dressed. "No time for make-up. I'll have to put it on later." She checked out of the hotel and was soon into her rental car.

While waiting to return the rental car, she prayed that she wouldn't miss her flight. Running through the airport she heard the announcement, "Last call for flight 335 for Los Angeles, boarding at Gate number 11. Please have your identification and boarding pass ready."

"Oh yeah, sure. I'll pull it out when I get to you," she said aloud. She finally reached the gate and reached into her bag for her boarding pass. To her surprise she couldn't find it. Her heartbeat sped up. "I don't believe this crap!" She threw her hands up in the air panicking, "I don't have time for this. She looked at the attendant. "I have to make this flight!"

The attendant said, "Miss, you need to take a deep breath so that you can calm down. Then check through your bag again."

"You don't understand! It's not…"

"Miss, calm down and recheck."

Sighing, she did as instructed. "Oh thank you God. Here it is." She handed it to the attendant.

"See I knew you would find it. Thank you for flying Northwest, have a safe flight." She smiled.

"Thank you." She closed her eyes and took another deep breath after being seated on the plane. Her nerves were really worked up from all the rushing around. "I can't wait to get home," she whispered.

"Rough morning?" the passenger next to her asked.

"You can say that. I almost missed my flight." Destiny noticed the program she was flipping through. Majestic's was on the top of the page. "Can I see that program?"

"Sure." She handed it over to Destiny. "By the way my name is Mya."

"Hi, Mya. I'm Destiny, nice to meet you."

"Likewise," Mya replied as she smiled at Destiny.

Destiny inhaled and exhaled slowly. "Are you heading to Los Angeles?" she asked while flipping through the program.

"Yes, I'm going to visit my family."

"So Mya, did you attend the opening of 'Majestic Hall'?" she asked while biting down on her bottom lip.

"No. I have a friend who attended. She brought me to the airport this morning and I borrowed the program. The owner is my cousin."

Renée's cousin, very interesting she thought to herself. "Oh. Why were you not invited?"

She frowned. "It's a long story that I'll rather not discuss."

Destiny could tell that something major had happened and their relationship had been affected by it. She would make it her business to find out what it was. This might just be my lucky day, she thought. She patted the back of her hand. "I understand. How long are you going to be in L.A.?"

"For about a month, then I have to get back to my husband and my son."

She pulled out her palm pilot to check her schedule for the next two weeks. "Would you like to go out to dinner one evening before you leave. I'll give you my number. I'm a model and I'm usually in and out a lot. If I don't answer, leave a message."

"Okay. That would be fine." She smiled and put her number in her purse.

A couple of weeks later Destiny decided to call Carla. "Hey Carla, what's going on?" she asked while lighting a cigarette.

"Girl, nothing. I'm just a little tired. I have a few days off so I'm going to catch up on my rest. I'm flying to Miami on

Thursday for a show. I have been on the move constantly for the last three weeks."

"How was your trip to Detroit?"

"It was good, but too short. I would have stayed longer if I didn't have that photo shoot the following day. The grand opening was off the hook. Renée has it going on. Anyone holding an event there will definitely not be disappointed. The hall is absolutely gorgeous."

She put out the cigarette. "Yeah, I know it is. I saw the…"

Carla raised a brow. "What did you say?"

"I said I'm sure it is gorgeous that is."

"You were talking as if you were there." She paused wondering if Destiny was really there. *Naw, she didn't have an invitation. There's no way she could have gotten in there.*

"You know I couldn't have been there. I'm sure it was by invitation only. Right?"

"Right."

Whew almost busted Destiny thought to herself. "I didn't get to spend any time with Jeremy."

"Yeah, I told Renée that I'd be back in a few weeks. Jeremy and I are going to hang out also."

"Did you talk to Ja'Ron about Jeremy yet?"

"No. I plan to do that when I go back."

"Are you still planning to do the charity event in Detroit?" Destiny asked.

"Yes. My contract has already been signed."

"Good. I've decided to do the event myself, so we'll be working together."

Trying to sound convincing, "Oh, that's going to be fun." For some reason though, she felt uneasy. Destiny was up to something, she was sure of that.

"Why did you decide to do the show, I know you don't like doing too many charity events."

"I'm changing as I age. I want to do more charity events" she lied. "It'll be fun to work a show with you again. Do you think Ja'Ron will be there?"

Carla frowned. "I haven't told him about it yet, so I don't know if he will be there or not." Carla knew that Ja'Ron would be there, especially since it was in Detroit.

"It'll be nice to see him and his little family." She smirked. "Sort of like a reunion." She laughed.

"I don't find that humorous Destiny. I'm warning you… leave Ja'Ron alone."

"I hear ya." She huffed and rolled her eyes.

"Destiny, please don't do anything stupid."

"Don't worry about it Carla, everything's cool. I'm going to hang up now. I have a dinner appointment tonight." She had talked to Mya a few times, to develop some type of relationship with her. Although, all she really wanted was to use her.

"Anyone I know?" Carla asked.

"No, I don't think so."

"I'll chat with you soon, Carla."

"Alright, bye."

"Hi, Mya. I'm so glad you could meet me."

"Oh, no problem. I told you I would before I left. I needed to get out of the house anyway. Thanks for inviting me."

They ordered their meal and Destiny went on and on about the different places she's experienced all over the world. "The glamorous world of modeling. So tell me about why you moved from L.A."

"I moved to Michigan to finish my master's degree. I lived with Renée until…" She turned her head. Guilt was written all over her face.

Destiny touched her hand. "What is it Mya? What happened that changed your relationship with your cousin? It's okay, your secret is safe with me."

She looked at Destiny with sadness in her eyes. "It's not a secret. Anyone who knows Renée or myself, knows the story." She paused. "I was attracted to her husband. I slept with him and got caught. Trust me it's nothing that I'm proud of either. I really hurt her and because of it, I've lost a wonderful person."

Destiny was shocked. "Oh my," was all she could manage. That was a blow. So Renée probably became very insecure after her loving husband cheated on her. "That's too bad." Now that she knew a little about Renée, she knew exactly which way to tackle her.

ELEVEN

The doorbell rang. "Punctual is he. I like that." She chuckled as she rushed to the door. Renee's smile quickly turned into a frown as she opened the door and recognized the unwelcomed face.

"Mya. What are you doing here?"

"Look Renée, I wanted to talk to you. It's been a few years now and I wanted to clear the air between us. You had done so much for me and I wanted to see if…"

Why couldn't she be as cold as Tiffany and slam the door in her face. "No need Mya. I forgive you for what you did. Actually you did me a favor. All that is behind me now and I've moved on with my life. Now if you'll excuse me, I have to prepare for my date. Good-bye Mya." She closed the door, inhaled and exhaled slowly. She went back upstairs to finish dressing. Fall was setting in, so she decided to wear a cable knit dress by Ralph Lauren, with a sexy pair of boots. As she pinned her hair up the doorbell rang again.

"I'll be right there," she screamed running down the stairs. Opening the door and gasping for air she managed, "Hi, Ja'Ron."

"Hi. You must have jogged downstairs."

She tilted her head, "Yes, I did."

"Are you almost ready?"

"Of course, I am."

"You might want to grab a jacket. It's a little cooler out today."

"Ok." She grabbed a jacket and locked up."

On the way to his house, they both discussed how their day went. She told him about her unexpected visitor. He pressed a button on his garage opener and pulled his Lexus SUV in beside a Candy Apple colored BMW.

She was curious. She had never seen him drive that car before. "Whose BMW is that?"

"Oh, that's Marsha's car. She loves her BMW's."

"Great, that means I'll get to see her and Jeremy."

"Wrong my dear. They are gone for a few days. She took the Jaguar." Sorry to disappoint you. It's just you and me. Is that ok with you?"

"Yeah, that's fine."

"I'm making dinner this evening," he announced as they left the garage and entered the kitchen. The room was a spacious all white and stainless steel room. The island in the center had built-in bookshelves, which were loaded with cookbooks.

Impressive, she thought. "I didn't know you could cook."

"I don't cook very often, but I can do a little something, something in the kitchen. My mom taught me how to cook. Everything's already prepped; I just have to finish up. Dinner will be done real soon. Would you like a glass of wine?"

"Sure."

"First, let me put your jacket away."

"Thanks. Would it be okay with you if I remove my shoes?"

"Sure make yourself at home. "Did you bring a pair slippers?"

She shook her head. "No. I didn't think of that."

"Don't worry about that, I took it upon myself to purchase you a pair. You probably wear a size 7 ½ right?"

She laughed. "Yeah, lucky guess." Dang, this man is amazing, she thought to herself. They went down into the basement, where she imagined he probably did his entertaining. There was a wet bar, a large screened television and a bathroom as large as a bedroom. She envisioned him and his boys hanging out down there. On the main floor was his living room, family room, the utility room, and his home office. There were four huge bedrooms, each with their own bathroom. "His home is very elegant," she muttered as he continued to show her around. As they traveled upstairs she was in awe when she saw the children's library room for Jeremy upstairs. A study table was located in the center of the room. There were wall- to- wall books, a section for children's video's, and a television in one corner. "Jeremy likes to read?"

"Yes, he does. Well, let's go check on dinner and I'll get you that glass of wine. You can sit in the family room if you like." She stopped.

"Is there something wrong?" he asked.

"No, just curious about the room."

"Oh, come on." He grabbed her by the hand. He opened the door and she gasped. He smirked knowing that he had her approval. They walked back down to the family room. Once he checked on dinner, he joined her. "Dinner will be done in a half hour."

"Great. Your home is beautiful."

"Thank you. I'm glad you like it." He smiled as he put an arm around her.

He had prepared a seafood salad complimented with lemon oil dressing. The main course consisted of lobster, lasagna, and broccoli. For desert they had lemon meringue pie. They ate dinner and retreated back into the family room. Ja'Ron put on some Jazz. He pulled Renée into his arms brushing his lips against hers. Desire instantly flooded her body as he gained entrance into her mouth. Her hands moved over the hard muscle of his chest, shoulder, and his back as their tongues entangled. His hands eased under the cable knit dress she wore. "I want to make love to you Renée," he whispered in a husky tone.

She nodded. "It's what I want also."

"Follow me." He took her upstairs and placed her on his bed. He unpinned her hair and it fell down her back. He began kissing her again. He ran his hands under the dress and pulled it over her head. He gasped, "You are so beautiful." He detached her lace bra and glared at her well-rounded breast. He began to suckle each breast.

She didn't want him to stop. "Mmmm…" escaped her throat. His tongued entered her mouth again and as he touched her center and she thought her body was going to explode.

"Baby, I need for you to understand that once we do this there's no turning back. We will belong to each other. I love you Renée. Are you ready for our adventure in life together."

She nodded. She couldn't deny it any longer; she was in love with him. "Um.. Ja'Ron."

"Yes, baby."

"I'm not on anything."

"Its okay sweetie, I'll protect us." He ripped open a condom and sheathed himself. He slid his tongue along her neck and she threw her head back and arched her back. Her hands explored every inch of him as he continued to torture her entire body.

"Ja'Ron… I haven't been with…"

"I know baby… don't worry, we'll take our time," he whispered.

She was ready to surrender totally to him. He slowly inched his way inside of her. Once inside, he took his time. She moaned in pure ecstasy. She matched his rhythm as their dance intensified. No one had ever made her feel this good before. Each stroke took her higher and higher until they both reached their peak. Tears rolled down her cheek. He held her close to him.

"I love you Renée." He kissed her damp forehead and collapsed beside her. "You're mine now, Ms. Colby. I'm never letting you go."

She smiled as he wiped away her tears and she curled up in his arms. She loved him too but decided not to let the words fall out of her mouth. *He is the perfect man,* she thought to herself.

TWELVE

Ja'Ron walked into Keith's office. He handed Keith a bagel and took his out of the bag. Biting into the bagel he announced, "Man, I'm ready to do this." Then he pulled out a velvet case from his briefcase.

"Do what Ja'Ron?" he asked grinning.

"I'm going to ask Renée to marry me this weekend. Go ahead, check it out, and tell me what you think." He rubbed his perfectly shaped goatee and smirked.

Keith opened the case. He playfully jerked back from the sparkles descending from the case. "Dang, bro."

"Well… what do you think? Do you think she'll like it? I would have liked to have gotten Tiffany's opinion, but I didn't want to take a chance on her telling Renée."

"What are you trying to say about my wife?"

He held up a hand. "I'm not saying she has a big mouth or anything, but you know how her and Renée are. Those two will get to talking and you know Tiffany might just spill the surprise." They both started laughing.

"I definitely think she'll like this. But I'm afraid you've created a larger problem.." He had a serious look on his face.

She looked at his friend curiously. "What's the problem?"

"Man, you know when Tiffany see this five carat diamond, she's gonna flip."

"That's your problem, not mine." They laughed again.

"Seriously though, I'm happy for you."

"Don't get too happy. She still has to say yes." He rubbed his goatee.

"I wouldn't worry about that, if I were you."

"Good afternoon ma'am, can I help you find anything?" Brandon asked while checking out the fine woman standing before him. *She looks familiar,* he thought. She wore a cream leather mini-dress, exposing her long beautiful legs, which were relaxed in a sexy sling back shoe. Her hair was shoulder length and straight. She had on a pair of Gucci sunglasses, which she slid to the top of her head once Brandon approached her to offer assistance.

"This is a pretty nice boutique here. Nicely laid out," she continued as she touched and admired the clothing lines Ja'Ron carried. "Cute he's even carrying children clothing," she murmured while frowning. She took in a deep breath as she gave Brandon her attention. "New place… how long have you been in this area?" She waited for a response as she turned to continue flicking through the clothing.

"For a few months now. Are you looking for something special?"

She pivoted and pasted a wide smile on her face. "As a matter of fact I am. I'm here to see Ja'Ron Moss."

"Mr. Moss is unavailable right now." Just as he said that, she noticed Renée walking toward them to leave the store.

"See you later Brandon," she said while waving.

See you later Brandon, Destiny mimicked under her breath.

"Alright Ms. Colby, you have a great day."

"Thanks I will."

"I can't stand that little prissy," Destiny said aloud.

Brandon questioned, "What was that?"

She noticed he was wearing a name tag. "Oh nothing, Brandon. Would you please see if Ja'Ron is available now?" She was getting a little annoyed.

"Yes. I'll see if he's available." He wondered why her mood suddenly changed.

"Thank you."

"Who should I tell him is here to see him?"

"Destiny Benstein."

"Destiny Benstein, the supermodel?"

"Yes, it's me."

"Wow! I thought you looked familiar. I don't believe it…I'm talking to Destiny Benstein. You're more beautiful in person. I see you in magazines. Oh, I can't believe it." He was going on and on. His babbling was beginning to pluck her nerves. She wanted to say, *whatever dude, just get Ja'Ron for me* but she decided against it. She simply smiled at him gloating all over her. She looked down at her watch. "Brandon, sweetheart I really need to see Ja'Ron. I don't have a lot of time."

"Oh, I'm sorry. I got so excited... well never mind. Let me check for you."

"Geek," she muttered with a fake smile. She turned her back to him.

Ja'Ron was sitting at his desk admiring a photo of Renée when his phone rang, "Mr. Moss, guess whose here?!"

"Who, Brandon?" He could tell Brandon was excited.

"The supermodel, Destiny Benstein."

He sat straight up in his chair. He couldn't have heard him correctly. His good day was clearly about to go downhill if he hadn't misunderstood what Brandon had just said. He scratched his head. "Who's here Brandon?"

"Destiny Benstein, and man she looks good."

Ja'Ron frowned. "What does she want?"

"She wants to see you. Why didn't you tell me that you knew her? Can you hook a brotha up?"

He couldn't believe his ears. It had been years since he saw her or even heard from her. "Brandon, please send Ms. Benstein in. Thank you." *What was she doing here,* he wondered.

She stopped at the restroom before going to his office. She had to make sure she looked her best. She applied a fresh coat of lipstick and muttered, "There, that should do it." She brushed her hair and flounced from the restroom right into his office, without knocking.

Some people will never change, he thought as soon as his door flew open. "Hello Destiny. How are you? I'm surprised to see you here." He hadn't moved from his seat to welcome her in.

"Hello Ja'Ron," she said as she swooped over to him and embraced him. He took a deep breath. She tried to kiss him on the lips, but he quickly turned his head. "What's wrong baby, aren't you happy to see me?" She plopped down on his desk.

"How have you been? It's been so long since I've seen you. You are still fine as…"

Ja'Ron shook his head and smirked. "I can clearly see that years haven't changed you any at all. Please get off of my desk. There are plenty of chairs for you to sit in."

"Oh Ja'Ron," she purred as she leaped from the desk. "I have changed a lot. I have a different outlook on life."

I bet you do, he thought as he watched her cross those long legs of hers. She pulled out a file and began filing her nails. He shook his head again. In an annoying tone he asked, "Destiny, what are you doing here?"

She wanted him to see a change in her so she had to maintain her cool. "Please don't use that annoying tone with me. I just wanted to talk to you."

His eyebrow rose, "About?"

She reached for his hand, but he quickly moved it. "Us Ja'Ron. I have come to realize that you are a special man and I'm terribly sorry for not trying to work things out with you before now. I want you back." Her eyes filled with water.

Oh no… not the tears, I'm not buying into that he thought as he watched her performance. He brought his hand up to his chin.

She continued, "I'm still in love with you and I want us to have another chance. Back then, I was so into myself and what I wanted until I didn't give you much consideration during our relationship. I know we wouldn't have made it years ago because of me. I wasn't willing to give you what you wanted, which was a family. But now, I'm successful and I want to settle down and have children… with you." She batted her eyes.

He burst out laughing. He stopped laughing, looked at her and started laughing again. He was struggling to gain control. "You've got to be kidding," he finally managed.

"No, I'm not kidding! I've kept tabs on you for the past few years. I know you haven't been really dating since you've had your nephew. I'm serious about this Ja'Ron. I didn't appreciate what I had before, but now I do. I really love you, I always have."

"That was touching, Destiny."

"Come on, I'm pouring out my heart to you, don't make fun of me," she whined.

"Look Destiny, I don't want to hurt your feelings but there's no way I would get back involved with you whether I'm dating or not. We're too different and I have moved on."

Her feelings were a little crushed but she wasn't going to give up. She stood up and adjusted her clothing. She did a pivot turn and walked toward the door. She looked over her shoulder and said, "I'll give you time to think about it. It was good seeing you and just remember that I'm not giving up on us." She smiled and walked out the door.

"This is a big joke. That woman has some nerves," he said while dialing his sister's number.

"Hello Carla."

"Hey bro. Whassup?"

"I don't know, you tell me. Your friend Destiny just left my office."

"What?!" Destiny was there?" She could feel a headache coming on.

"Surprised Carla. Well so was I when she came waltzing in here."

"What did she want?"

He started laughing.

"Ja'Ron, what's so funny? What did Destiny want?"

"A reconciliation is what she wants. Isn't that the most ridiculous thing you have heard in a while."

"Yes, it is. I had no idea she was in Detroit. That girl is a trip."

"You don't have to tell me she's a trip. Since we're on the subject of Destiny, why didn't you tell me she was in New York when we were there a few months ago?"

"How did you know she was here? Did she tell you that?"

"No, she didn't tell me. Jeremy was playing a video game that I hadn't bought. I asked him where he had gotten it from and he told me from Aunt Carla's friend, Destiny."

"Oh yeah, I forgot all about that." *Good Lord, what is Destiny up to*, she wondered. "So she wanted to reconcile, huh? What did you tell her?"

"After I finished laughing at her pouring out her soul, I told her there's no way I would even consider it."

"How did she take it?"

"I don't know and don't care. I just wanted her out of my office. After all these years, she's got some nerves. Enough breath wasted on Destiny. I have some good news."

She was grateful for the change in subject. "What's that?"

"I'm going to ask Renée to marry me this weekend."

"Cool, I know she'll say yes. You two are so wonderful together."

"I hope you're right about her saying yes."

"She loves you, I can tell. Well bro, I would love to talk to you longer, but I have to get ready for an appointment. I'll see you in a couple of weeks. By the way Ja'Ron, I better mention that Destiny is also modeling for the charity event in Detroit."

"Great. I don't have a problem with that. I just hope she doesn't try and start any trouble. Renée and I are still coming."

"Cool. Love ya, I'll talk to you later. Bye."

"I'm going to kill her!" Carla screamed aloud after she hung up the phone. She had to reach her before she did any damage. She dialed her cell phone number but there was no answer. Although she figured she probably wouldn't return her call, she left her a message anyway. "Unbelievable. I have to stop her from trying to ruin Ja'Ron's life. She'll go after Renée next, if Ja'Ron doesn't give in."

Destiny pulled herself together for her next stop. "You won't be laughing for long Ja'Ron," she proclaimed as she stepped out of the car. She marched into Renée's Bridal Boutique.

"Hi, may I help you?" Jessica asked.

"Yes, I'm here to see Renée Colby."

"Hmm…" Renée wasn't in and she hadn't mentioned canceling any appointments. She checked the appointment book and found nothing scheduled for this time of the day. "What's your name ma'am?"

"Destiny Benstein."

"Did you have an appointment with Ms. Colby?"

"No, I didn't." She rolled her eyes and huffed under her breath.

"Ms. Colby only does consultations by appointment."

She was losing her patience. "What is with you people?!"

"Excuse me," Jessica said placing a hand on her hip. Potential client or not, she was not about to allow this woman to speak to her any kind of way.

"I'm sorry, I'm not having a good day. Look... right now I don't live here, but I will be soon. I want her to hire her to be my wedding consultant. I hear she's the best. I need to talk to her as soon as possible." She placed her left hand on the counter exposing a three carat diamond. She turned around when she heard the store's door open and there Renée was. She walked over to her as if they had known each other for years. "Hi Ms. Colby, my name is Destiny and I'm in a tight bind." She placed an arm around her. "I'm getting married and…"

Jessica interrupted. "Renée, I was just explaining to her that she will need to make an appointment."

Destiny threw her hand up and waved her off. Jessica shot her an *I know you didn't look*. She was tired of this brat's rude behavior.

"It's okay Jessica, I'll take care of this."

She glanced at the time. "Look, Destiny I have an appointment in twenty minutes I need to prepare for. I'll be more than happy to assist you, but I just cannot take a walk-in appointment. My schedule simply will not allow it. If you cannot wait, then I'll be more than happy to refer you to someone else."

"No, I want everything arranged by you and your staff. I'll make an appointment. I'm sorry about all the fuss."

"No problem, you can give Jessica the information we need. Have a great day."

She gave Jessica her name and a phone number to contact her at. Her appointment wasn't for another couple of weeks. She figured she would have to stay in town a few days after the charity event, but it would be worth it. She had to get Renée out of the picture so that she could secure Ja'Ron for herself.

The restaurant was crowded. "Maybe, we should dine somewhere else," Renée suggested.

"No, this is where I want to dine tonight if you don't mind the wait."

"No problem. I don't mind the wait at all." She looked around and noticed several people waiting to be seated.

He pulled the greeter to the side and whispered something to him. They waited five more minutes before being seated. Ja'Ron chuckled. "See, it helps when you know the owner."

She shook her head and replied, "What am I going to do with you?"

"Hmm… Do you really want me to answer that?"

"Watch it Mr. Moss." They enjoyed their dinner and right after desert was brought to the table Ja'Ron stood up and asked for everyone's attention.

She looked around. She whispered, "What are you doing Ja'Ron?"

"Trust me baby, it'll be okay." She placed one hand against her head and sat there unsure of what was going on. "Tonight I'm dining with the most beautiful woman in the world. I fell in love with her the first day I laid eyes on her." He glared into her sparkling eyes. She closed her eyes realizing what was happening. She reopened them and they were filled with tears. "Renée, I couldn't imagine spending my life without you," Ja'Ron said on bending knee. He pulled out the velvet box and opened it.

"Wow!" the on looking guest exclaimed as the diamond lit up the room.

"You are so special to me." He stroked her beautiful cheek. She was overwhelmed with joy. "I Love You Renée, will you marry me?" She threw a hand over her mouth and the tears rolled down her face.

The guest shouted, "And your answer is?"

"Yes," she said. "Yes. I will marry you." He placed the five-carat diamond on her left finger and they kissed as though no one else was in the room. The waiter cleared his throat and tapped Ja'Ron on the shoulder.

The guest clapped and shouted "Congratulations!"

On the way to her house she thought about how happy she's been since her and Ja'Ron began dating. She was excited about beginning her life with him and Jeremy. She suddenly felt compelled to know what his viewpoint was on her working. She turned to him, "I hope you don't expect me to give up my business once we're married."

He wouldn't have even suggested that she give up her dream. "Not at all sweetheart. That wouldn't be fair for me to ask you to do that. However, you'll always have the option of giving it up whenever you want to and if you want to. The decision will be yours to make."

She felt relieved hearing this because Robert had given her a hard time and made her feel guilty about fulfilling her dreams. He didn't support her wanting this business very much at all. "So when we begin having children, that's not going to be a problem either, right?"

"That's right. We will do whatever necessary to make sure we are both satisfied. I promise you that."

Upon locking the door to the house Ja'Ron swept her into his arms and carried her to her bedroom. After an intensified lovemaking session she said, "I love you so much Ja'Ron. I'd given up on love until I met you."

"Sweetheart, my love for you is strong and I know that we can endure anything together." He kissed her forehead.

"So Ms. Colby, when are we going to set a date?" He tapped her on the nose. "No long engagement either."

"How about the weekend before Christmas."

He shrugged and shook his head. "I don't think so. That's too long."

"No it's not, that's less than three months away. Nothing is booked for that weekend at Majestic's either. That's perfect."

"Ok. I guess I can't wait until you become my wife." He embraced her.

She looked up at him. "Did Tiffany know about this?"

"Do you think I'm crazy. You know she wouldn't have kept that to herself. I wanted it to be a surprise." They laughed. "Keith knows though."

"What about Jeremy? Is he okay with this?"

"Yes, you know he loves you as much as I do. I asked him how he would like for us to be a family. He's excited about having a mommy. Carla sends her congrats also."

"And Marsha?"

"Marsha is very excited. She said it was about time. She also said we better hurry up and give her some more grandbabies to spoil before she gets too old."

"She's right you know." She looked at her ring again. I cannot explain the joy I have right now. "This ring is so beautiful."

"Nothing but the best for you. I'm glad you liked it."

"I love it, but not as much as I love you." She snuggled up against him and fell asleep.

Tiffany walked into Renée's office finding her going through some contracts. Tiffany plopped down on the couch. "Girl, I'm so tired. I'm not working all day today." She leaned back on the couch and closed her eyes. She reopened them and looked over at Renée. "Renée, you're glowing."

Renée waved her hand at her. "Shut up Tiffany, you're just tired. Your eyes are deceiving you." She continued going through her papers.

Tiffany thought she saw a sparkle, but then she dismissed it. "Yeah you're right, my eyes are deceiving me. Plus, I'm hungry, let's go get something to eat before I go home."

"Tired and hungry. You're pathetic. Oh by the way, we have another wedding reception scheduled for the week before Christmas."

Tiffany stretched and yawned before standing up. "Ok. We'll talk about it tomorrow. Right now all I want to do is eat and get in my bed."

Renée placed her laptop and her papers into her briefcase. "Come on Tiffany, lets go. What do you want to eat?"

"Shrimp, lobster and fish."

"Alright to Red Lobster we go."

"Dang girl, did you eat today? You were hungry," Renée said while watching her friend chow down. "You better be careful not to gain too much weight. It'll be hard to shed the pounds after the baby is born. You know how you are."

"I know, I haven't gained that much weight. My doctor said since I'm all stomach, I should be fine."

They had almost finished their meal before Tiffany noticed the sparkle again. She looked curiously at Renée again.

"What?" Renée asked while finishing her drink.

"Something's up with you."

"Why you say that?"

"That glow. The sparkle. Are you pregnant?"

She laughed. "I don't think so."

She glared her friend in her twinkling eyes. Renée, don't play with me. Spill it… Spill it right now!"

She started laughing again. "Girl, you've been seriously tripping lately. We'll blame it on the changing hormones."

"Hormones, huh?" She knew she was in love but she had a different glow today. If she's not pregnant, what could it be she wondered? She said aloud, "The sparkle, I wasn't that tired. That's it! Let me see your hand." She motioned for her to honor the request.

Renée held out her right hand.

Tiffany sighed and frowned. "The other one please."

Renée held out her left hand and…

She gasped at the size. "Dang, girl!" Renée thought Tiffany's eyes were going to pop out of her head.

"Now that's what I call a big, flawless rock. Ja'Ron gave you that! Why didn't you tell me?"

"I was just waiting to see how long it would take you to notice. I deliberately flashed it every once in a while, but you hadn't figured it out until now."

All of a sudden Tiffany burst out crying. Renée looked confused. "Are you upset about this?" The tears were unexpected. "Tiffany, what's wrong sweetie"?

"Nothing. It's just that I'm so happy for you."

"Now you stop that crying before you make me cry."

After moments of tears, she dried her eyes. "You two have found true love and I'm truly overjoyed."

"I owe this all to you and Keith. If I hadn't come to the Hawaiian party, we may not have met. Thank you Tiffany." She paused for a moment. "I am so happy. The wedding that's scheduled the weekend before Christmas is mine and Ja'Ron's."

Tiffany got up and gave her friend a big hug and a kiss. "I knew this would happen, remember what I told you months ago. Seeing you happy is all I want. Everything's perfect now."

"Yes it is," Renée responded with a smile.

THIRTEEN

She had rechecked the listing with her agent before arriving to Detroit and Destiny's name was not listed as one of the participating models. She called Destiny, but each time she received no answer. She was kind of happy that Destiny's name was not included, however, for some reason she was feeling a little nervous tonight. The charity event had begun and she still hadn't reached Destiny. She put on her first attire for the evening, inhaled a deep breath and exhaled slowly before stepping out onto the catwalk.

Carla was relieved when the show was over and she was glad that it had gone well. She quickly changed into her own clothing and joined the table where her family was seated. People were leaving but they decided to chill out for a little while. They were sitting there enjoying great conversation when…

"Hi everyone!" Carla felt kinks in her neck and chills ran down her spine as she turned to face the familiar voice. Ja'Ron smile quickly turned into a frown. Renée looked confused, remembering the woman had been in her shop a few weeks ago. *What's the connection Renée wondered?* Tiffany and Keith just looked at the sudden mood changes in the Moss family since the highly energized woman approached the table.

"Oh my God, please don't let this night be a disaster," Carla softly prayed. "Destiny, what are you doing here? I guess you changed your mind about participating in the show, huh?"

"Yes, Carla I did, but I didn't change my mind about coming." Her speech was beginning to slur.

"Destiny, I think you've had too much to drink. Where are you staying? I'll drive you there."

"Oh no you don't, Carla. I'm not leaving until I get what I came here for." Everyone's attention was on Carla.

"What's going on Carla?" Ja'Ron asked with agitation in his voice.

"Yeah Carla, tell him what's going on," Destiny demanded as she walked over toward Ja'Ron and Renée. "So Ms. Colby, I see you have met my groom already." She walked around the table flashing her left hand so the entire table could see the ring. Carla shook her head and slowly sunk in her chair.

Renée was puzzled but she was determined not to jump to any conclusions. She calmly asked, "Who are you referring to Destiny?"

Ja'Ron whispered, "How do you know Destiny?"

"She was in my shop a few weeks ago demanding to see me. I didn't have time to sit down and consult with her then, so I told her to make an appointment. She's suppose to come in on Monday so we can begin her wedding plans."

Ja'Ron shook his head. "Oh my God, Renée don't ask any questions right now. I'm asking you to trust me. I want you and Tiffany to leave the room."

"No, I'm not leaving without you."

His eyes had turned cold. "Please just do as I ask."

"What's wrong Ja'Ron?" Renée asked. She didn't know what to make of this weird situation. She was not going anywhere. She was getting upset. "You can't just shoo me out of here!"

He was angry. Renée had never seen this side of him. Ja'Ron demanded, "Tiffany get Renée out of here so that I can deal with this – now!"

Keith turned to Tiffany. "No time for questions, just do as he has requested. Take her home and I'll come and get you later."

"C'mon Renée, let him deal with this."

Tiffany and Renée stood up to leave. Renée was very angry by now. Destiny noticed the big rock sparkling on Renée's finger. Her temper began to rise. "Where do you think you're going? You tramp... you stole my man!"

Renée walked over to her and slapped her across the face. "I've had enough of your stank attitude. Who in the…"

Destiny cut her off as she pulled away from Renée. "Ja'Ron is going to marry me and there's nothing you can do about it. Carla you better tell the lovely lady."

Carla pointed a finger at Destiny. "I warned you not to do this Destiny! Will you please shut up? You're drunk and you don't know what you're saying or doing."

She placed her hands on her hips. "No, I won't shut up until I'm done!" Renée, he ain't gonna marry you because he wants to be with me. You see we're going to be a family. We…"

"That's enough Destiny!" Carla shouted.

Ja'Ron interrupted. "Who told you I wanted to be with you Destiny. You haven't changed, you're still as selfish as ever and I don't appreciate you disrespecting…"

She stopped him by slapping his face. "That bratty kid you've been taking care of is my son, not Carla's. When you broke up with me, I was pregnant. Instead of having an abortion, Carla talked me into having it. I hate kids, but you will not gain custody of him unless you marry me!" She was irate and out of control. "I intend for you to suffer! There will be no happy life for you unless I say so. That is if you want the kid to remain with you." She giggled. "So whose having the last laugh now Ja'Ron, huh? Whose laughing now, baby?"

The whole room was at a standstill. No one moved. All mouths were dropped except for Destiny's and Carla's. Carla put her head down and wept. Destiny was full of laughter. "Kiss your little prissy good-bye Ja'Ron. You will finally be mine."

Renée couldn't believe her ears. "This can't be happening!" She looked over at Ja'Ron while removing the engagement ring. She threw it at him and ran out of the room in tears. Tiffany followed right behind her. Ja'Ron sat back down, obviously in shock. A million things were going through his head.

Keith sighed as he grabbed the chair next to him. "What a mess!" he whispered.

"Tell me about it." Ja'Ron managed as he turned his attention toward his sister. She sat there knowing that she deserved anything he dished out to her right now. She had made a very big mistake. "So Carla, what do you have to say about all of this?" She sat there in silence. " Why didn't you tell me? You are just as pathetic as your trifling friend. You two are a piece of work."

The tears flowed like a river down her face. She didn't know what to say to him. "Did you get a kick out of watching me take care of Jeremy, not knowing that he was really my son? No wonder you didn't want him calling you mommy." He stroked his chin and shook his head. "You came waltzing here year after year, knowing the truth but decided not to say anything. Did you even consider my feelings?" He slammed his hand on the table. "Say something Carla! This is not the time to be lost for words!"

She was shaking as the tears continued to flow. "I'm so sorry Ja'Ron. I really am. At first I was honestly willing to take care of him myself."

"Why didn't you tell me she was pregnant with my child? All of this could have been avoided! I would have taken him from her as soon as he was born. Was your friendship more important to you?"

"No, it wasn't. She threatened to have an abortion if I mentioned a word to you about her being pregnant. I didn't want her to abort, so in order for her to have him I had to agree to keeping my mouth shut. I knew she didn't want a child, so I also agreed to take him. After I realized I couldn't give him the time he deserved, I decided to bring him to you. You were more stable and that way you would know him also. I know this all sounds crazy, but I tried to do the right thing for Jeremy's sake. You've got to believe me!" She paused. "I know you don't want to hear this right now but, I named him Jeremy because I remembered when we were growing up that you said that's what you wanted your first son's name to be. I'm so sorry you had to find out this way. I really didn't mean to hurt you or him. I love both of you so much."

He saw the sincerity in her eyes as he sat there processing every word she spoke. "I'm not sure if I can forgive you for what you have done."

"You can reach me at this number," Destiny announced to Ja'Ron as she threw him the piece of paper. "Don't make me wait too long or I'll come and take back my kid." She turned to leave the room.

Ja'Ron grabbed her by the arm. "You better stay away from him. I will not allow you to hurt him in any type of way. I have enough witnesses here who heard you declare your hatred for kids. I will be in touch with you, but you can believe that it won't be for any type of reconciliation. I don't want you." He smirked. "Who would? You're worse than you were years ago. You make me so sick! You will never get him back, I promise you that. Now you listen and you listen to me good, you will sign over all parental rights to me before you leave town." He let go of her arm and she stampeded from the room.

FOURTEEN

Ja'Ron telephoned Marsha the following morning to let her know what had happened. She insisted that it would be best if she kept Jeremy away for a few days.

He paced the floor as he held Renée's ring in his hand. He had attempted to get some work done but he couldn't. He needed to talk to Renée. He loved her but he was unsure of the damage that Destiny may have caused. He had phoned her several times, but she hadn't returned any of his phone calls. His pacing continued when he heard the doorbell ring. He ran to the door hoping that maybe it was Renée.

"Hey man, how are you?" Keith asked as he walked in.

"I'm making it." He sighed as he poured them something to drink. "I just hope I haven't lost Renée due to this mess. I haven't been able to reach her. Has Tiffany mentioned anything at all?"

"All I can suggest is that if you really love her, you better let her know it. Her and Tiffany did leave town for a few days."

"Should Tiffany even be traveling? I've finally found the love of my life and this had to happen. She's probably thinking that I'm going to take Destiny back in order to keep Jeremy, but that will never happen. I have to find her and talk to her. Where are they?"

Keith shook his head. "Tiffany cleared everything with the doctor before leaving, so she will be fine." He paused. "As for where they went, I can't tell you. I promised Renée that I wouldn't. I'm sorry man." He patted him on the shoulder, understanding his pain and his need to reach her. "She just needs some time to sort everything out. In the meantime, you need to get this custody thing settled with Destiny."

"She's going to be here for the rest of the week. Do you think you can draw the papers up before she leaves?"

"Sure. I knew you would want them so I got everything ready and brought them with me today. Do you think she's just going to give you what you want?"

"Absolutely! There's no doubt in my mind, and she'll do it without a fight. I guarantee you that."

"How's Carla?"

He shrugged. "I don't know and right now I don't care."

"I understand you being angry Ja'Ron, but she is your sister. And although she went about things the wrong way, I really do believe that she cares. She could have let Destiny abort the baby, but she knew that you wouldn't have wanted that to happen. Jeremy doesn't know any differently. Although you thought he was your nephew, you have been raising him like he was your son. Actually, it was good thinking on Carla's part not to confuse him with thinking that she was his mom. So as far as Jeremy is concerned, your relationship and his relationship with his aunt haven't changed. You know how strongly you feel about family so you need to try and work things out with Carla. Don't let this split you all up."

"I'll think about it. I'm not making any promises though." He rubbed his chin. "I'm supposed to leave town next week for a couple of days, but I might cancel."

"No, you go ahead. I think getting away would be a good idea."

"Do you think Renée will be back when I return?"

"Yes, they'll be back by then. You know they are both protective of each other. Tiffany just wanted to get her out of the area for a few days."

Ja'Ron reclined back into the lazy boy and rubbed his forehead. "Things were going so great for us. She had let down her guard and I had gained her trust. She loves me as much as I love her. It would have taken that manipulative Destiny to show back up and attempt to destroy me. But she will not win. I will not lose Renée or my son because of this!"

Renée tossed and turned most of the night. She decided to get up and check her messages. Ja'Ron had left several messages on her home, business, and cell phone every day since she had been gone. She hadn't returned any of his calls because she needed time to think things thoroughly. She wasn't quite sure if she was ready to deal with him just yet, besides she had given him his ring back. Finding out that Destiny was Jeremy's mother had definitely changed things. Although she knew that Ja'Ron loves her, she knew how important it was for a child to have both parents in the same home. That was one reason why she suddenly divorced Robert after finding out that Mya was pregnant with his child. She wanted him to be free to be with his child on a daily basis, if he chose to do so. She could tell that Ja'Ron didn't have any feelings for Destiny, but she couldn't ignore her threat to take Jeremy away from him if he didn't marry her. Renée loved Ja'Ron and wanted to be with him, but right now the right thing to do was to let him go. She would have to move forward with her life without him.

When Tiffany awakened she would insist that they return back home today. They had planned to stay a couple more days, but she did have a business to run and the Bostic's wedding was the next big event to be held at Majestic's. She looked over at her best friend. "I'm so blessed to have such a wonderful friend," she whispered as she watched her sleep. They had endured plenty of hard times together.

She entered the bathroom to run a hot bath in the Jacuzzi. She pinned her hair up and sank down into the water. She closed her eyes and tried to focus on anything except for Ja'Ron, but it wasn't working. She envisioned the pain that he must be in right now and she was sorry that she could not be there for him. She felt that it would be best for everyone if she stayed out of the way. Tears began to roll down her face. "I had finally found true love and this had to happen. I love him so much," she mumbled. She wiped her face and pulled herself together. She quietly prayed, "God, please help me to get through this and get over him."

"Renée. Renée, where are you?" Tiffany asked as she rose from the bed.

"I'm in the bathroom Tiffany."

Tiffany stood at the door. "Are you okay?"

"Yes, I'm fine. I was thinking earlier that we should go back home today. We have to make sure everything's in order for the Bostic's wedding. Besides, you need to get back home to your husband. I know you two are missing each other."

"Ok. If you're sure you're ready to go back then that's fine with me. I do miss Keith, but I want you to be ready to return. As far as the wedding goes everything's ready and right on schedule. I talked to Shantell and Jessica on yesterday. And of course you know Fonso has his end under control. The bridal party picked up their gowns and accessories on the day we left. Jessica said that the bride was extremely impressed with the gown that Patti created for her. This is going to be an extravagant event. I can't wait to see the eyes of the guest once everything begins." Tiffany then called her husband to let him know that they would be returning today. Before they hung up he filled her in on what was going on with the Moss family.

They took their seats on the plane. Tiffany had settled in and she munched on some fresh fruit. "You want some Renée?"

"No, you go ahead and feed our baby." She smirked at her friend. "Girl, you know you can eat."

Tiffany drank her juice and wiped her mouth. She had been careful the last few days not to mention too much about Ja'Ron, but now it was time to talk about it. She knew that Ja'Ron was not going to give up on Renée, but she needed to know what her friend was thinking about the entire situation. "So, what are you going to do about Ja'Ron?" Tiffany questioned.

"There's nothing for me to do Tiffany. I'm not going to be the cause of him losing his son. I will free him, just as I freed Robert to do the right thing for his son."

"Renée, he loves you not Destiny. He's not going to marry her, I can promise you that."

"You don't know that Tiffany. It doesn't matter if he marries her or not, I'm not going to be the cause of him losing Jeremy. He loves Jeremy too much." She let out a frustrated sigh. "Let's not talk about this right now. I need to focus on other things." She pulled out her organizer to check her appointments for the week. Jessica had rescheduled her appointments for the next two days. She felt relieved because that would give her some time to get back into the swing of things.

Tiffany detected the pain in her voice and decided not to push her to continue the conversation. She felt that their getaway to Chicago helped Renée somewhat not to totally focus on what had happened a few nights ago. They both enjoyed shopping for the baby while in Chicago. "Keith finished the nursery while we were away."

Renée smiled at her while placing her organizer back into her briefcase. "I know you're happy about that. The baby will be here real soon. I can't wait to spoil him or her." Someday, she wanted to be where Tiffany was today – planning for a new arrival. She felt a little sad because she was getting closer to that day and all it took was a big secret to shatter everything. *Oh well life goes on,* she mumbled silently to herself.

Renée walked into her house and begin to unpack when her phone rang. She decided not to answer the call.

"Hi Renée, its Ja'Ron. I hope you had a safe trip. I truly understand the reason for you leaving town for a few days. I'm sorry that things went down the way that they did, but we need to talk about what happened and our future. I understand you not returning my calls, but there will come a time real soon when you will have to face me again. I will not allow you to run from away me. I'm out of town right now but I'll be back on Friday. We need to get together then. I love you and you best believe I'm not letting Destiny's trifling ways or anyone else come between us. I'll talk to you soon. Bye."

She continued to unpack. She decided to go to her office when she finished. She telephoned Jessica to see if she could stay a little later this evening to go over whatever she had missed the past few days. Jessica didn't know exactly why they had suddenly left town, but she knew it had to be something serious. After speaking with Jessica she rode over to the office.

"How are things Jessica?" Renée questioned as she walked through the door.

"Great. How are things with you?"

"I'm fine. Any messages or anything unusual happen while I was away."

"Nope, nothing really unusual. I rescheduled all of your consultations except for one. The bride couldn't wait until you got back so I started that one myself and informed the her that she would have to finish up with you."

Both of Renée's eyebrows shot up. "What's the bride's name?"

"Oh, you'll remember her I'm sure. It was none other than the snotty little Ms. Destiny Benstein."

"What?!" Renée was instantly pissed. "Destiny came back here."

"Yeah and she left a two thousand dollar deposit to secure her wedding date."

Renée brought both hands up to her face and shook her head. She couldn't believe her ears. "She must be crazy if she thinks that I'm doing any business with her. I don't care how much she's willing to spend."

"What's going on Renée? I've never heard you refuse to work with any bride, no matter how difficult they could be."

"I know Jessica. Let me break it down like this. Destiny and Ja'Ron have a child together and she's threaten to take the child from him if he doesn't marry her."

Jessica looked confused. "Where is the child? You couldn't be talking about Jeremy. Are you?"

Renée nodded.

"Oh my God. I'm so sorry Renée."

"It's okay Jessica. I'll be fine. Did Ms. Benstein leave a phone number where she could be reached?"

"Yes. Do you want me to contact her?"

"No, I'll take care of it." She proceeded to her office.
"Oh Renée, I forgot to tell you…"

Renée opened her office door and Carla was sitting there waiting for her. She quietly chuckled in disbelief. She muttered, "What now?" Coming to the office this evening was a definite mistake. "Hello Carla." She closed her door and walked over to her desk.

"Hi Renée. I was here when you called Jessica earlier, so I begged her to let me stay until you got here. I know that I'm the last person you probably want to see right now but I had to talk to you. Ja'Ron doesn't even know that I'm in town. I figured you would be back in a week so I cancelled all of my upcoming events for the next two weeks. I feel responsible for screwing things up for you and Ja'Ron. I'm so sorry. I never meant for this to happen. I had not seen him so happy about being with any woman like he has been since meeting you. He loves you, Jeremy loves you and I love you too. I'm just here to beg you not to let Destiny destroy what you two could have together."

"I appreciate you coming Carla, but it's not about what me or Ja'Ron wants anymore. He has to do what is right for his son since his real mother has shown up. Jeremy deserves to be raised by both of his parents. I love all of you all to that's why I'm willing to let Ja'Ron go so that his son won't be robbed being raised by both of his parents."

"But he doesn't love her and she definitely doesn't love him. He's not going to marry her just because she's Jeremy's mom. He won't allow her to trap him. That goes against his integrity. Ja'Ron didn't buy her that ring that she had on."

"Where did she get it from then?"

"She bought it herself."

"That's ridiculous. You mean to tell me that she's went through all this trouble and she doesn't love him."

"Yes, she doesn't want him to be happy. She'll never stay with him and Jeremy because she doesn't even like children. She would never be a good wife or a good mother. That's one of the reasons why her and Ja'Ron are not together today. She tried to fake wanting the same things that he wanted; but he soon found out the real truth. Everything was all about her. She never wanted the family that he has always wanted. When she told me she was pregnant, I could hardly believe it. I know I went about things the wrong way, but at least I was able to convince her not to abort Jeremy." She paused, taking a deep breath. "Somehow she managed to meet your cousin Mya."

Renée eyebrows shot up and she frowned. "She met Mya, where?"

"On the airplane going back to California. Destiny was actually at the opening of Majestic's, but I just found that out."

"Mya wasn't at the opening, and how did Destiny get in?"

"She slipped in when no one was paying attention."

"Hmm... I'll have to tighten that. No one should have been able to get in without an invitation." She made a note to discuss that with Tiffany. "Go ahead."

"Well anyway, Mya wasn't there but had managed to get a program from someone. Destiny noticed it on the plane and struck a conversation with her. Mya told her that you two were relatives and she was visiting her mom in California. Destiny talked her into having dinner with her before she left. She used Mya to get all the information she needed on you and your ex-husband. She knows that Ja'Ron doesn't want her. She also knew how you felt about a child having both parents in the home, so she counted on you reacting the way that you did. Destiny confessed everything to me the next day after the charity event."

Renée looked out of her office window. "That conniving, manipulating little witch!" She was pissed. "How could someone be so cruel?" She shook her head in disbelief. "Well I can't deal with this until after the Bostic's wedding is over. All of my energy has to be focused on that right now."

"I understand. Well I have to be going now." She turned around before exiting from the room. "Renée, please promise me that you won't tell Ja'Ron that I came here."

"Ok. I promise." They embraced. "Take care Carla."

All of this excitement in the last few hours had worn her out. She gathered her things and went home.

FIFTEEN

Ja'Ron was exhausted when he returned home from his trip. No one was home so he figured he could get a short nap in before Jeremy came back. He checked his messages, hoping that Renée had called. He was disappointed to find out that she hadn't. Carla on the other hand had left several messages. He had given what she had done much thought and had forgiven her in his own heart, but he had decided not to talk with her just yet. His main focus right now was reconciling with Renée and making her his wife. He took a quick shower and slipped into bed. He was sleeping good until he heard his bedroom door swing open.

"Daddy's back Nana!"

Marsha came to the door. "Come out of there Jeremy, let him get some rest. Remember how tired I told you he would probably be?"

Ja'Ron gave him a welcoming smile. "It's okay Marsha, I need to get up anyway."

"Alright Ja'Ron, welcome back home." She left the room.

"Hey squirt, come here and tell daddy what you've been up to." Jeremy jumped onto the king size bed and began chattering away. Ja'Ron had missed him. He just smiled as he listened to him chatter and was thankful that he was his son. Destiny had signed off all parental rights to him and he was grateful that she hadn't given him a difficult time about it. Once Jeremy took a break from talking, Ja'Ron pulled him close to him and began tickling him. He was laughing and kicking until tears ran down his face. "Did you know that you are a very special little boy and your dad loves you very much?"

Jeremy looked at him with those bright brown eyes. "Yes, dad and I love you too. When are you and Renée getting married again?"

Ja'Ron thought for a moment before answering him. "Right before Christmas, sweetheart."

"I love her too daddy."

"I know squirt, so do I. So do I." He had to make things right with her. "What would you like to do tonight, Jeremy?"

"Umm… go to the movies. Is Renée coming too?"

Jeremy was not making this any easier with all the questions he thought as he rubbed his chin. "No, she won't be able to come with us tonight. It's just you and me kid."

"Oh yeah dad, Aunt Carla called and she wants me to come visit her one weekend. She said she had to make sure it was okay with you first. Can I please go?"

"We'll see Jeremy. I haven't talked to her about that yet." She did love Jeremy and he knew that so he wouldn't dare keep him away from her. But Jeremy would not go to New York if Destiny was there, and he would make sure that Carla understood that. He had explained to Destiny that she is not going to be a part of Jeremy's life for now. Once Jeremy is older, if he wanted to have a relationship with her that would be up to him. For now, he didn't want her trying to corrupt Jeremy in any way. "I'm getting up now and getting dressed. You go and change your clothing and we'll head out to dinner and then to the movies."

Carla paced her living room floor contemplating whether she should call her brother or not. How long would he not speak to her. She went up to her room to lie across her bed. She looked over at the photo on her nightstand. "Mom and dad, I wish you were here. I have done a terrible thing and I don't know when or even if Ja'Ron will forgive me." She began to cry. "I thought I was doing the right thing, but everything has blown up in my face. I'm so sorry that I hurt him." The phone rang but she didn't want to talk to anyone so she rolled over and decided to let the answering machine do its job.

"Hello, Carla it's me Ja'Ron. I know that…"

She suddenly felt a burst of energy flow through her body as she raced to pick up the receiver before he hung up. "Ja'Ron."

"Yes, its me Carla."

"I'm so happy to hear your voice."

"What's wrong Carla, have you been crying?"

"Nothing will ever be right again if you don't forgive me for what I did."

"You're forgiven. You're my sister and I love you no matter what. But please, no more secrets or surprises like this. I'm just grateful that everything turned out okay after all."

"So you managed to get Destiny to sign off parental rights?"

"Yes, Keith rushed things and she willingly signed off her rights. So I take it you haven't talked to her."

"Not since we were both in Detroit. Have you spoken with Renée?"

"No, she hasn't returned any of my phone calls. I'm not giving up on her though."

"She still loves you, you know."

"I need to hear that from her. She's going to have to face me sooner or later."

"How's Jeremy?"

"He's fine and he said he wants to come to New York one weekend."

"I would like for him to but I didn't know if you would let him just yet."

"Just so you know, if Destiny is going to be there he's not coming. I mean that Carla. If I find out he's been around her without my knowledge in advance that will cut off any visits to New York without Marsha or myself. Do you understand me?"

"Yes, loud and clear. Believe me when I say I have truly learned a big lesson from all of this. I will not do anything against your wishes. I promise."

"Good. Well sis I'm going to let you go. Now you should be able to rest, I forgive you and I love you very much. Bye."

"I love you too. Bye."

SIXTEEN

A few weeks had passed and the day had come to unveil the big fairy tale wedding. Renée started up her car and headed to Majestic's. She began to think about Ja'Ron. He had called several times and sent flowers to her, but she had given him no response. She had decided to wait until after the Bostic's wedding to contact him. The brother of Celeste Bostic spent a fortune to make her day a memorable one. Renée wanted this day to be absolutely flawless. She invested a lot of time and energy into this wedding. Celeste was going to be a gorgeous bride, no doubt about it. Renée was thankful that the rehearsal had been successful and everyone was very cooperative. She was exhausted but she enjoyed every minute of planning Celeste's wedding. Besides that, it was the first themed wedding they had planned. The invitations were in the form of a storybook inviting guest to join in this magical union of the bride and the groom. Enclosed in each storybook was a gold-tassel bookmark. Also they had included a note inviting the ladies to wear ball gowns and the men to wear formal attire. As soon as she got to Majestic's she would have Fonso make her a cup of coffee. She needed some caffeine.

The trees on the outside of Majestic's were decorated with long flowing ribbons. There were mice statues surrounding the carriages on each side of the hall. "Beautiful," she whispered to herself. Renée and Tiffany made their rounds to make sure everything was in place. Inside the ballroom was the scene of a palace. A backdrop was hung with a painting of a winding staircase. There were several grandfather clocks in the ballroom with all hands stopped at midnight. Life-size wired sculptures wrapped with sparkling lights were around the room. A pumpkin coach, a fairy godmother, and a glass slipper were other accessories created for the occasion. Hanging from the ceiling above the head table were colorful flag banners. The chairs were covered with royal colors: purple, emerald green, or gold. The tables were covered with floor-length white tablecloths and gathered overlays. The centerpieces were velvet pillows with gold braiding and tassels, each holding a glass slipper, which were filled with roses. For favors each guest had a box of chocolates that looked like storybooks with 'Once Upon a Time" inscribed on each one. Also, for each guest, lay a program with a castle on front. Inside a brief story was told on how the bride and groom met and a little history of their lives so far. Following that was the program for the evening. For the guest book the guest wrote their names with a large feather quill pen on the pages of an oversized fairy-tale book.

"Everything looks great!" exclaimed Tiffany. "Let's go check on Fonso and his staff." The fruit and cheese were bountiful and beautiful around the ice sculpture of a glass slipper. Ham, roasted leg of lamb, and turkey would be served along with a variety of salads, potato and rice dishes. Fonso designed a castle-shaped cake and ice cream swirled with honey and sunflower seeds would be served along with that for dessert. The groom's cake was a storybook entitled "Once Upon a Time." Along with that he also made chocolate slippers, which were filled with mousse or berries. Shantell came into the kitchen to notify them of the bride's entrance. Tiffany went to check on her while Renée drank a cup of coffee. "My goodness, this wedding has drained me."

The music began to play and the groom entered the room dressed like a prince. He wore a velvet doublet, covering a white shirt with ballooning over sleeves. He wore puffed out breeches and hose. On his feet he wore above the ankle pointed toe shoes made of soft leather. And of course he wore a crown. The groomsmen were dressed similar to the groom, substituting the crown with velvet - plumed hats. The bridesmaids were dressed in straight gowns. Their hair was braided with flowers accessorized throughout the braid. They carried a small bouquet of lilies.

The flower girl wore a peasant-style dress with a white, square-neck chemise, laced bodice and a tattered-edge skirt. She wore a handkerchief-scarf head covering. She carried a wood-looking pail filled with rose petals, which she scattered along the bridal path. The ring bearer costume was similar to the groom's. He carried the rings in a glass-looking slipper placed upon a red velvet pillow adorned with gold braiding and tassels.

The bells began to ring notifying the guest of the bride's arrival. The dark brown skinned twenty –one year old was stunning. The guest were in awe. She wore a Renaissance designed gown. The bodice was tight fitting with silk and gold cording accents. The waist was Basque. The sleeves were Juliet styled sleeves. The flowing skirt had padded hips and a slit in the front to show the under skirting. The cathedral train hung from the shoulders. She wore a sparkling tiara. And of course she wore clear slippers. Her bridal bouquet was an arrangement of gold roses, gardenias, and lilies, accented with a hint of pearls and tiny sparkling faux jewels.

To begin the exchange of the wedding vows the bride's fairy godmother lightly tapped her head. Once the couple were pronounced husband and wife white doves were released. The entire evening was a delight for everyone who witnessed it. Renée and Tiffany received an enormous amount of compliments from the guest. Everything had turned out perfectly as planned.

Renée was definitely exhausted. She wanted to get home and sink comfortably into her bed. After the amount of hard work she had endured the past few weeks, rest was well overdue.

Tiffany approached her. "Is something wrong Renée," Tiffany asked?

"No, why?" She was hoping the fatigue wasn't showing.

"You look like you are not feeling well."

"I'm fine, just a little tired from the evening. I'm going to go…"

"Renée, Renée, answer me Renée. Oh my God!" She began to shake her. She looked around the hall. All of the guest were gone, but some of the staff were still there. She screamed. "Somebody help me!" Jessica and Shantell came running toward them. "Call 911. Hurry!" Tiffany checked to make sure Renée still had a pulse. "Renée, hold on sweetie. Help is on the way." She closed her eyes and prayed that her friend would be okay.

Jessica came back with a blanket for Renée. "An ambulance is on its way Tiffany. Is there anything else you want me to do?" She laid the blanket on top of Renée. Tiffany held her in her arms.

"Jessica, go grab my cell phone from the office and call Keith and tell him what happened and tell him to meet me at the hospital."

Shantell walked up. "Is she going to be okay?"

Tiffany lowered her head and smoothed down Renée's hair. "I hope so, I really do hope so."

Jessica said, "I'm going to call Keith now, and I'll bring your purse to you. Do you want me to get Renée's also?"

"Yes, I'll need her insurance information. Thanks."

Renée began to move around. At first everything was a blur to her. Then she realized she was lying on the floor.

"Renée honey, just lie still."

"What happened Tiffany?"

"You passed out and an ambulance will be here shortly."

"I'm fine Tiff, I think that I just need some rest."

"You might be right, but you're getting checked out anyway by a physician."

The ambulance arrived and the paramedics checked her vitals. "Ma'am your vitals are stable, but we would like to take you in for further observations."

"That's fine," Tiffany replied.

Keith joined them at the hospital and waited with Tiffany to hear Renée's test results. He had thought about calling Ja'Ron to let him know what had happened. Then he decided against it once Tiffany had informed him that Renée had not spoken with him since the charity event. The doctor entered the room and asked Renée if she wanted her friends to remain with her while he discussed her results. "Is it that bad?" she asked.

"No, not at all. You're in good health actually," the doctor replied.

She sighed. "Good. They can stay." She knew that Tiffany would not leave without a fight anyway.

"Well Ms. Colby, you and your friend have something in common."

Renée gave him a puzzled look. "Who are you referring to and what exactly are you suggesting here?"

The doctor looked at her with a beautiful smile on her face. "As I was saying, you're in good health, but I recommend you slow down a little bit because you're pregnant."

Both of her eyebrows were raised, eyes widen, and her mouth dropped. She looked over at Keith and Tiffany and they also had a beautiful smile on their face. Tiffany reached over to her and kissed her on the cheek. "This is wonderful. Our babies will grow up together." She rubbed her belly.

Renée was in shock. She knew that she hadn't just heard the results of her test correctly. It took her a few moments to respond. "I can't be, not now!" She shook her head in disbelief. "This is the worse timing for this news." She had given Ja'Ron back his ring and hadn't spoken to him since the charity event. She had spoken with Carla, but what if he reconsidered marrying Jeremy's mother. *What a mess*, her mind suddenly screamed. She closed her eyes, turned on her side, and began to cry.

"Ms. Colby, are you going to be okay? There are other options if you don't…"

Tiffany frowned and quickly interrupted. "Don't even let that fall from your lips, doctor. She'll be fine." She turned to her friend, "She's in shock, just give me a few moments to talk with her."

"Okay. She can be discharged whenever she feels like leaving. Just inform the nurse and she'll get her discharge papers. Make sure she makes an appointment with her physician soon and make sure she rest for a few days."

"Alright, thank you."

Renée awakened early the next morning to the sound of the doorbell ringing like crazy. She looked over at the clock; it was

9:00 a.m. "Oh… Who could be here this early in the morning?" Suddenly her heart rate increased. "What if its Ja'Ron? I can't talk to him right now." She peeked out her bedroom window to see whose car was in the driveway. She released a huge sigh and was thankful to see the royal blue Jag sitting outside. "Why didn't Tiffany just use her key?" The doorbell rang again as she grabbed her robe to go downstairs.

"Morning, Tiffany." She yawned. "Why are you up so early on a Sunday morning? I know you haven't had much sleep," she said recalling the previous night's events. " I was planning to sleep in today, you should have done the same."

"I had to take Keith to the airport this morning. Instead of going home, I decided to stop by here." She marched her cute little pregnant self into the kitchen.

"I didn't know Keith was going out of town. How long will he be gone?"

She shrugged her shoulders. "For a couple of days." She pulled two glasses from the cabinet and poured them some orange juice.

"Let me go put on some clothes and we can make us some breakfast."

"Sounds good to me."

The kitchen was soon filled with the aroma of sausage and bacon. They also made hotcakes and eggs. Renée cut up some cantaloupe, strawberries, and fresh pineapples. They had prepared a feast for themselves. They both set the table and sat down to chow down. Renée started laughing.

"What's so funny, Renée."

"We cooked as if we were serving a few hungry people."

Tiffany smirked. "We are silly. We are feeding ourselves and our babies." She took a sip of her orange juice. "I'm so excited about our babies growing up together. I just hope that they are as close as we are."

Renée's smile ceased and she suddenly didn't feel hungry anymore.

"Renée, what's your problem? Ja'Ron is going to be so happy when he finds out that you're pregnant. You are planning to tell him soon…right?"

"I don't know Tiffany…I don't know." She brought her hand up to her cheek.

"You have to tell him. Do you recall the big surprise we all got a few weeks ago. You wouldn't dare do that to him, would you?"

"But what if he's already committed to Destiny?"

Tiffany huffed. "I seriously doubt that has happened. He loves you, not Destiny. He's been trying to reach you for weeks now; you're the one who is avoiding him. What are you really afraid of right now, at this moment?"

"I know Ja'Ron wants a family, but what if I can't give it to him. What if I have another miscarriage?"

"Then you two would still have Jeremy."

She ran her fingers through her hair. "That's the other thing. What if she takes Jeremy from him because of me and then I lose this baby." She rubbed her stomach. "This is not how I wanted things to turn out."

Tiffany raised her brow as she placed another hotcake onto her plate. "It doesn't matter now, does it? What you need to do now is talk to the man you love. It's not all about you anymore."

Renée released an exhausted sigh. "You're right, the sooner the better." They cleaned the kitchen and they both decided to take a little nap.

SEVENTEEN

Renée took a day off work to rest, but she was determined to return back to her business the following day. Tiffany had stayed the night and awakened her before she left for work that morning. Renée had been unable to fall right back to sleep. She was missing Jeremy and his daddy terribly. She was tempted to call Ja'Ron but quickly decided against it. Flipping through the channels, she sighed, unable to find anything worth watching. She got up and cooked her some breakfast before retreating back to the bed. She finally drifted off to sleep.

The dream began, *She carried the baby full term and had given birth to a beautiful baby girl. She had decided not to tell Ja'Ron about the pregnancy. She avoided him and eventually he stopped trying to reach her. It was best that way. She had refused to discuss or listen to anything about him. As far as she knew, he had reconciled with Destiny. She didn't want to interfere; her and her baby girl would be just fine. She hated the fact that Jeremy might not know his sister though. Tiffany was with her during the delivery. She had been the perfect coach. Once the baby was cleaned up Tiffany handed the baby to her.*

"Isn't she beautiful?" Tiffany asked.

The proud mother smiled. "Yes, she is." She had long curly jet-black hair. Her skin was a beautiful golden brown color. Renée began to check her out to make sure she had all of her fingers and toes. "She's perfect."

Tiffany smiled as the baby opened her eyes. "Hello precious, it's me Aunt Tiffany. Welcome to your new world. We have been patiently waiting for your arrival." She looked at Renée. "She looks just like her daddy. Her beautiful brown eyes, nose, and her mouth. How long will you deprive him of knowing her?"

"Don't start Tiffany."

"This isn't fair Renée and you know it. Look at her. If he saw her, he would know that she's his child. I don't know or care if he is with Destiny; he had the right to know about her. I didn't

push the issue before because I wanted you to have a stress free pregnancy, but now you have to do the right thing."

Renée rolled her eyes and grumbled. *"The right thing for who?" We will be fine. I'm capable of taking care of her myself."* She pulled her baby girl close to her chest.

Tiffany was getting upset with her. She huffed. "You have to do the right thing for her and her father!" Her dream was interrupted when she heard the telephone ring. She reached over to answer it but paused when she heard the voice on the line. The answering machine picked up.

"Hi Renée, its Ja'Ron. I hope all is well with you." Her stomach began doing somersaults. "I've been trying to reach you for weeks now. You cannot and will not continue to brush me off. I have given you some time to think about things and now its time for us to talk. I would appreciate it if you would call me to set up a time that's good for you. I look forward to hearing from you." He paused. "Today."

"Humph… who does he think he is?" She looked down at her stomach and closed her eyes. "He has some nerves, I ain't calling him until I get good and ready." She got up, did some light cleaning, and then watched television for the rest of the day.

Renée began her drive to work. The sun was shining brightly. "It's a beautiful day today." She stopped to get doughnuts and bagels with cream cheese. She felt good and refreshed this morning.

She placed the goodies on the table in the lounge. "Good morning, Jessica."

"Good morning. I'm glad you brought in breakfast today," she continued while grabbing a bagel. "Thank you. Are you feeling better?"

"Yes, I'm fine."

"What did the doctor say?"

She smirked while removing a doughnut from the box. "Take it easy and get more rest."

"Yeah, you have been really overdoing it for the past few weeks." She pointed to a beautiful arrangement sitting on the table, "Those came for you this morning. Celeste's wedding was a huge success. The phone is still ringing off the hook as a result. I booked a couple of appointments, and the rest of the calls were compliments from several attending guest."

She offered Jessica a winning smile. "That's great! I'm going to my office now. Let me know when Tiffany gets in." She grabbed a bagel and the vase, which held the bouquet of flowers.

"Okay. I will."

Renée opened her office door and gasped when she saw who was there. She wanted to leap into his arms. She felt his gaze burning throughout her body.

He was admiring every inch of her. The lavender colored pantsuit was perfectly fitting in all the right places. Her face was glowing. He wanted to reach out and grab her but decided that the time was not right for that. "Hello Renée. Please allow me to get that for you." He grabbed her briefcase and placed it beside her desk.

She was surprised and glad to see him. Butterflies were fluttering around in her stomach. Her heart was jumping for joy, but instead of allowing herself to show it she gave him an annoying look. "Hello Ja'Ron. What are you doing here?"

"We need to talk Renée and since you are refusing to return my calls, I decided to stop by."

"We have nothing to talk…"

He could no longer resist. He kissed her hard and demanding. Her body was aching for more. "I love you Renée."

She looked into his sincere eyes, but quickly turned her head. She loved him too. "I need for you to leave. I have a ton of work to catch up on."

He sat down. "I'm not leaving until we talk."

She frowned. "We can't talk here, not today."

"Well, will you at least agree to dinner tonight?" He was determined to get that engagement ring back on her finger.

She sighed and shook her head. "You don't give up, do you?"

"You should know the answer to that by now. So what's it gonna be?"

She silently huffed. "Okay. I'll join you for dinner tonight. What time and where?"

"Does seven work for you? And as far as where, you don't need that information because I'm picking you up."

She stood and placed her hands on her hips. "Oh really!"

"Really. I want to make sure you don't stand me up."

She grumbled. "Then seven is fine."

"I'll see you then. Have a great day." He kissed her cheek and left the room.

"You too." She gazed for several minutes at the flowers before placing her head on the desk. "What am I going to do?"

"What are you going to do about what Renée?"

Her head quickly rose up. "Tiffany I didn't know you were already here. I wasn't expecting you this early. I asked Jessica to let me know when you arrived."

Jessica placed her juice on the desk and began to spread cream cheese on her bagel. "Well girlfriend, I'm waiting."

She shifted in her chair as Tiffany took a seat. "When I walked into my office this morning, Ja'Ron was waiting for me."

Tiffany lifted her palm upward, while nodding. "And."

She nonchalantly shrugged her shoulders. "He's taking me out to dinner later and I guess we'll talk."

"You're going to tell him about the baby, right?"

"I don't know if I'll tell him just yet."

"Renée. Don't do this to yourself or him. You two love each other. Whatever doubts you are having, I'm sure you two can work it out together. And you know he's not the one to beat around the bush."

"Yes, I do know that to be true. Well I better get to work so that I can get out of here on time." She chuckled. "Did anything come up yesterday which needs immediate attention?"

"Not that I can think of. I spent most of the day over at the hall." She smacked herself on the forehead. "I almost forgot, I'll be right back." Tiffany quickly wobbled from the room.

She returned shortly with a gift bag in her hand. "Celeste's brother came by the hall yesterday to bring us a thank you card, a box of chocolates, and an expensive bottle of wine. I didn't leave yours in your office yesterday when I stopped here briefly, so here you go." She handed Renée the bag.

"Thanks. That was nice of him, he didn't have to do this."

"That's what I told him. He said he was more than happy to do it. He appreciated all the time we put into making Celeste's special day one to remember. He said that his family was amazed with our work. All that money he spent, he must really love her."

Renée held up the bottle. "I guess it'll be a while before this bottle gets opened."

"You got that right," she agreed while rubbing her stomach. They laughed. "You didn't answer my question earlier, missy. You are going to tell him tonight, right?"

"We'll see."

Renée finished up earlier than she had expected. She found herself driving in the direction of Ja'Ron's boutique. She was sitting at the traffic light, getting ready to turn into his parking lot when she noticed him embracing a woman. She couldn't believe her eyes when she recognized who the woman was. "Destiny! Uh... uh," she continued as she gripped the wheel tightly. "I'll show him." The cars behind her were honking their horns. She checked the lane to the right of her for clearance. She quickly jetted over and drove straight home. She thought about the dream she had the day before. "That's it, its really over," she said while running a warm bath. "Men! They're all the same old dirty dogs. They want the nice and the naughty women too. That's not happening here, not again in this lifetime."

EIGHTEEN

"What is taking her so long to come to the door? This is not like her." He had called, but got no answer. He was beginning to worry that something had happened to her. He rang the doorbell again.

"Okay. Okay." She cracked the door open. "I changed my mind, I'm not going."

"What! Why?"

"It doesn't matter anymore. Just forget you ever met me. We can't be together." She closed the door and leaned against it allowing the tears to freely flow.

He got back into his car and just sat there stunned. She had responded somewhat to him earlier. "What in the world was going on with her?" He didn't know, but he was determined to find out. He was not going to lose her and that was a promise. He knew exactly who would have the information he needed. A few days later he called Tiffany.

"Hi Tiffany, how are you?"

"I'm fine Ja'Ron. What's happening? I was on my way out the door."

"I don't know. I was hoping that you could tell me. I need to talk to you about Renée."

"Oh." She hadn't been to work in a few days and hadn't talked with Renée since Ja'Ron had come by the office. "So, how did your dinner turn out?"

"It didn't. I went by her house to pick her up and she refused to go. She wouldn't even let me in the front door."

"Really?!" She wondered what had gotten into her friend. She seemed relaxed about going to dinner with him.

"Yes, really. That's why I'm calling you. I hate to get you involved in this, but I need to know what's bugging her. Then I'll have to figure out what to do next. So would you be willing to help a brotha out? How about lunch today?"

"Sure, what time? You know I ain't turning down a free meal."

"About eleven-thirty, I'll pick you up if that's okay with you."

"That's fine. And don't worry I won't mention this to Renée. I'll be waiting at the boutique for you."

"Thank you."

"You're welcome."

Tiffany wobbled into Renée's office. "Hey, Renée," she said sinking down into the couch.

"Whassup, girly? You're not looking too good today."

"I'm fine," she responded not looking up from her desk. "I just have a lot on my mind that's all."

"I'm going to be out for a few hours today. I'll be leaving around eleven."

"That's fine." She still made no eye contact.

"How did it go with Ja'Ron the other night?"

She gave her friend an annoying look. "I didn't go with him."

"Why not?"

"Because I didn't want to, ok" she said with an attitude.

"You seemed like you wanted to earlier that day. What happened?"

She stared at Tiffany without blinking. "I drove by his boutique and who did I see locked in his arms?"

Tiffany shrugged her shoulders. "I don't know, who?"

"Destiny."

"Destiny?" she questioned. "Are you sure?"

"I couldn't mistake her for anyone else, even if I wanted to."

"Oh Renée, you're probably overreacting. Even if she was in his arms, it most likely didn't mean anything. I can't believe you just jumped to conclusions like that. It's so unlike you."

"It doesn't matter. It's best if I just let go. He's no different from Robert."

"Oh now, that's cold. He doesn't deserve to be compared to Robert. Have you considered asking him about it?"

"It doesn't matter. End of discussion!" She started typing on the computer.

"Okay, if you say so. I'm sorry if I upset you. I hope you're in a better mood when I return." Tiffany left the room. Now she had to find out what game, if any, Ja'Ron was playing.

"Man, is she ever pissed off at you," she said as she took a bite of fettuccine. "Mmmm... this is so good."

"What did I do? I thought she was finally ready to talk about everything. I arrived at her house, and it was like..." He shook his head. "I don't know what happened. I know I had planned to put that ring back on her finger that night. Now I don't know what to do to reach her. But one thing I do know for sure is that I'm not giving up on her." He was very agitated. "She's the woman for me, I can't just let her go."

"What about Destiny?"

"What about her?" Then the desperate actions Destiny had taken haunted him. "Renée doesn't see Destiny as a threat to me and her, does she?"

"Wouldn't you, if the shoes were on the other foot?" She finished off the garlic bread.

"Oh, no. I've been trying to reach her and tell her she has nothing to worry about, but she's making it very difficult by not allowing me to."

Tiffany was curious. "So you're not marrying Destiny?"

He started laughing. "Absolutely not!" He began to wonder if Keith had mentioned any of their conversations since the charity event. Probably not he concluded remembering that Keith has been on the go for the past few weeks.

"Renée told me that she saw you embracing her the day you came by the office."

"That's absurd." He chuckled.

Tiffany didn't find anything humorous. "So are you calling her a liar?" She raised an eyebrow, ready to defend Renée to the fullest if he was insinuating that she had lied.

He took a drink of water and thought about what she could have seen before responding. He then thought about that day. He walked Destiny out to her rental car and they said their good-byes. "Renée was at the boutique that day?" He didn't recall seeing her.

"You tell me."

"Destiny came by to apologize, that's all. I walked her to her car and…"

"And what Ja'Ron? Don't get speechless on me now."

"We said our good-byes and she hugged me, but I didn't embrace her back. She put her arms around me so quick, I didn't have time to stop her. That must have been what Renée saw."

"Whew!" She sighed. "Boy, you had me worried there for a minute. You two have a lot to discuss. I'll try to scheme up a way to get you two together. In the meantime try not to contact her. I'll handle the rest."

"Thank you, sweetheart. I don't know how I could ever repay you for this."

"You're going to have a hard time trying to repay this favor. Especially if it works." They both laughed as they exited the restaurant.

The following weekend Tiffany managed to get Renée to agree to go on an overnight trip with her. They shopped all day and returned to the hotel that evening. When Renée stepped into the hotel room, she found Ja'Ron sitting at the desk. Her heartbeat palpitated. She turned to Tiffany. "What's going on? What is he doing here?"

"Don't get mad Renée, but you two need to talk. Keith is here also, call me if you need me. Love you." She slammed the door shut and went to find her husband.

"I love you Renée and we're going to talk this out right here, right now."

She shook her head. "Okay. What is it you have to say?"

"First of all, I want you to know that Destiny has no place in my life."

She grunted as she shifted in the chair across from him. She suddenly felt as if she was going to faint. "Please excuse me for a moment." She went into the bathroom and splashed her face with cool water. "Dear God, please don't let me get sick now," she silently prayed. She pulled herself together and slid back into the chair across from him.

"Are you okay?" he asked.

"Yeah, I'm just a little tired. Proceed."

"I'm not marrying Destiny."

"But she'll take Jeremy from you. I don't want that to happen."

His heart melted knowing now that her biggest concern was for Jeremy. "She's given me full custody of him. She has no parental rights. Everything was concluded the day you saw me in the parking lot of the boutique with her."

"Oh!" She felt a bit foolish. "Well, I guess I owe you an apology. I placed you in the same boat as my ex. I should have given you a chance to explain everything and for that I'm sorry."

"Your apology will be accepted under one condition."

Her brow rose. "And that condition would be?"

He stood up and retrieved something from his over night bag. "Renée Colby, will you marry me?"

"Yes, Ja'Ron Moss I will." He placed the engagement ring on her finger. He then smothered her with an intoxicating tender kiss. His lips slid down her slender neck caressing her with slow seductive kisses. She pulled back. "I have a surprise for you too."

"I'm waiting."

Tears began to fill her eyes. "What's wrong Renée?"

"Can we sit down first?"

"Sure." He sat beside her on the bed and held her hand.

"What is it… baby?"

"That's it."

"What's it?" Ja'Ron looked confused.

"I'm pregnant."

He was speechless at first. "What did you say?" His beautiful brown eyes widen as he waited for her to repeat what she had just said.

"We're going to have a baby."

He was filled with joy. As he began to undress her, he drove his tongue deeply into her mouth. She moaned as he cupped her full breast into his hands and began to suckle them one by one. His hands were prancing all over her body. His tongue burned her body from head to toe. Sparks shot through her entire body. She missed him and wanted him inside of her now. He ripped off his clothing and he tested her gem for readiness. She splayed her legs and he slowly entered her. They began to dance an enchanted dance. Their rhythm was matched to perfection. He lifted her hips to him as he drove deeper into her intoxicating sweet walls. She was almost at her peak and he was definitely there. One, two, and three, both of their bodies exploded in pure ecstasy together. She shuddered underneath him. The sweat ran down his face. "Woman, you have made me a happy man. The wedding date is only a few weeks away. You and Tiffany have some quick planning to do."

NINETEEN

Renée took a hot shower and dressed in her jogging suit. After pulling her hair in a ponytail she proceeded downstairs to take a morning walk. The rehearsal dinner was scheduled for tonight. Tiffany and Carla were handling everything and she was more than happy to allow them to do just that. All Renée and Ja'Ron had to do was show up. She grabbed her house keys and placed them in her pocket. As she walked around the block she thanked God for bringing her and Ja'Ron together. She also thanked God for giving her the ability to love again and for her love to be returned more than she could ever have imagined. She then rubbed her tummy and thanked God for her unborn child and prayed that he or she would be healthy.

Renée glanced down at her watch. "I better hurry home before Patti shows up." Patti was dropping off her evening dress for the rehearsal dinner tonight. She turned the corner leading back to her home and suddenly she felt like she was either being followed or watched. She stopped and turned around but no one was in sight. "Humph…pre-wedding jitters, I suppose." She shook her head and continued home. As she turned the doorknob to enter her home, she heard the phone ringing. "Maybe it's Ja'Ron," she said.

She hurried to over to take the call but the caller had already hung up without leaving a message. After checking the caller ID, she concluded it was probably a telemarketer or someone with the wrong number since it had shown up as an unknown caller. About five minutes later the phone rang again. "Hello." The person on the other end didn't say anything. "Hello," Renée said again without receiving any response. "I don't have time to play games," she said before hanging up the phone. She looked at the caller ID and the call was unknown. She walked into the kitchen to fix herself something to eat. The phone rang again and she glanced at the caller ID and she was glad that it was her husband to be.

After completing their conversation she called Patti to see if she was on her way. Renée was in the process of leaving a message when the doorbell rang. She walked over to the door with the phone in her hand. "Hey Patti, I was just leaving you a message." She hit the end button on her phone. "Come on in."

"Hi, sweetie. I'm sorry I'm late. And I apologize for not calling."

"Oh, it's not a problem at all," Renée said as she slowly closed the door." They walked in the kitchen. "You want something to drink." She scanned the refrigerator. "I have orange, grape, and apple juice. There's lemonade, Pepsi, and Sprite. I also have milk."

"Is that all? I don't know what I'm going to do with you and Tiffany." They both started laughing.

"Pepsi is fine. I had a customer come in just as I was preparing to leave. I thought I would never get rid of her."

"You know I can understand that. You want ice or not?"

"A couple of cubes would be fine. Thanks."

She handed Patti a glass of Pepsi and they headed into the family room. "Well let's see what you've got." Patti unzipped the garment bag and pulled out the dress. Renée shook her head, "It's absolutely gorgeous, Patti." The red dress was strapless and trimmed with a narrow band of sparkly clear rhinestone gems. The back was open with criss-cross lacing. The lower back zipped up. To complete the look of sophistication, she made a matching wrap / shawl. Renée purchased a pair of clear sling back heels to wear with the dress, and Tiffany had purchased a beautiful pair of earrings for her to wear.

"Go ahead and try it on. Holler if you need help with the zipper."

"I think I can manage, but I'll let you know if I can't."

Patti smiled when she came back into the room. "You look beautiful."

"Thank you for everything, Patti. I love this dress and I know that Ja'Ron will love it as well."

"You're welcome, sweetie. I'm going to go now. I still have a few things to do before the dinner tonight. I'll see you later on okay."

"Ok." After Patti left, Renée decided to take a little nap. The phone ringing awakened her. Still not fully awake to reach for the phone, the answering machine picked up. "Hi Renée, this is Destiny. I really do need to speak with you as soon as possible. Please call me at…" Renée rubbed her eyes, hoping that she was dreaming. She got up and walked over to the machine and sure enough she had a message. After replaying the message, she decided not to return the call. Then she thought about her walk that morning and feeling like she was being followed, then she remembered the phone call earlier. "It must have been her. What could she possibly want now?" Renée questioned. She shook her head and sighed. "No drama, not today."

She picked up the phone and called Tiffany and told her about the phone call.

"What? Is she in town?"

"Yes. The number was local."

"Don't call her back – I mean it Renée. Did you tell Ja'Ron?"

"No, I didn't and I'm not going to either. I don't want to upset him."

"Well, he's going to be upset if you don't tell him. You have to tell him."

"Alright. But I will not mention it until after the rehearsal dinner."

"Oh my, I'm going to be late for my own rehearsal dinner. I need to call Tiffany and let her know that I'm on my way." She picked up the phone and there was no dial tone. "Hello."

"Hello Renée, please don't hang up."

She recognized the voice immediately. "Look Destiny, I don't have time to chat right now. I'm already running late for an engagement."

"Please Renée, just give me a moment."

"What is it now, Destiny?"

"Would you meet me in the morning at Starbucks. I just need to talk with you. It will not take long, I promise."

"Ok. Ten-thirty."

"Thanks Renée, thank you so much."

Jessica and Shantell were assisting with the rehearsal and the wedding. Carla had just informed them that Renée hadn't arrived as of yet. "Tiffany, where's Renée?" Ja'Ron questioned. "She's already fifteen minutes late. That's not like her. I called her cell phone but I didn't get an answer. What if she's sick or what if something has happened to her?"

"Nothing's happened to her. If she's not here in five minutes…"

A bubbly Renée bounced in. "Hi everyone, sorry I'm late." Ja'Ron turned around and glared at his beautiful fiancée. He sighed with relief that she was there. She stood there smiling, as her guest sat there amazed at her appearance. The red gown was a knockout. And the look on Ja'Ron's face was priceless.

Nia and Regina's mouths were dropped. Nia spoke up, "My, my, my… If she looks like that tonight, what in the heck is she going to drop on us the day of the wedding? Look at that glow she has?"

"Dang, I hope I look that good when I get ready to walk down the aisle," Regina said.

Nia smiled as she continued to check out the gown. "She hasn't even walked down the aisle yet Regina."

"You know what I mean." Regina drank a sip of her wine.

Ja'Ron walked over to her. He kissed her softly on the lips. "You are exquisite. I love this gown."

"Thanks."

"Are you okay?" he questioned.

"Yes, I'm fine. Is everyone here and ready to begin?"

"Yes, we were just waiting for you. Why were you late?"

"I'll explain later. Let's get started." Once the wedding rehearsal was over, dinner was served. Everything had gone well and Ja'Ron and Renée were very happy. "Everyone did a wonderful job tonight didn't they Ja'Ron?"

"Yes, they did. I'm glad you allowed Tiffany and Carla to handle things for tonight."

"Yeah, me too."

"Daddy and Renée, how did I do tonight? Are you proud of me?

"Yes, we're proud of you." Ja'Ron said.

"And you did an excellent job tonight," Renée added. "Did you enjoy the dinner?"

"Yes, it was delicious. Guess what guys?"

"What?" Ja'Ron and Renée asked together.

" Nana's taking me home now. I'm so tired," Jeremy said.

"Ok squirt, give daddy a hug good night." He reached down to embrace his son. Then Jeremy gave Renée a nice big hug and a kiss on the cheek. "I love you," he whispered.

"And I love you too, Jeremy."

"Marsha, are you guys going to your place or ours?"

"I'm taking him to my place since it's the closest. I'm exhausted. I think Carla mentioned something about coming to my place also."

"That's fine. I'll be at Renée's tonight if you need anything."

"Ok. I'll see you tomorrow. Good night Renée. Make sure you get you some rest tonight." She rubbed Renée's cheek.

"Yes, I'll do that. Good night Marsha, and thanks for everything."

"You're more than welcome sweetheart." She smiled and gave her a hug. Marsha and Jeremy then proceeded to the car.

" Just think in a couple of days, we'll be husband and wife." She sighed as she laid her head against his shoulder. "I'm exhausted."

"I'm driving you home tonight. I'll bring you to your car in the morning."

She was too tired to argue with him. "Ok. I have a ten-thirty appointment in the morning."

"That's fine." They thanked everyone and left.

Renée left a message for Tiffany letting her know that she was on her way to meet with Destiny at Starbucks. Renée was dreading meeting with Destiny, but at the same time she was curious as to what she wanted. "Thanks for meeting me Renée."

"You're welcome. Destiny, why are you here?"

"Look, I wanted to apologize for everything that I put you through. I was wrong and I hope that one day you can forgive me for it."

"I forgive you. But is that really why you came back?"

"No. I need your help with something."

Renée raised a brow. "My help…with what?"

"Jeremy." She held her head down for a moment. "I know I haven't been any type of mother to him, but I would like to change that if at all possible."

She could feel her pain. What type of woman would put her career before her own child? Jeremy is such a loving and respectable little guy. Who could ask for anything more? She knew that she would never do that to Jeremy or any other children that her and Ja'Ron brought into this world. "What is it you think that I can do for you Destiny?"

She sighed and water was filling in her eyes. "Would you please talk to Ja'Ron? I just want to be able to see Jeremy sometimes."

"I really don't know, Destiny."

Tears began to fall. "I know that you're the only one who can get him to change his mind. I'm begging you." Tears were rolling down her cheek.

Renée reached into her purse and pulled out a small package of tissues. She handed them to Destiny. "I'm not making any promises, but I will talk to him."

"Thanks Renée. Oh yeah, this is for you and Ja'Ron. Please accept it. It's the least that I can do. I'm really happy that he has truly found someone who can love him and give him what he deserves." She smiled. "He deserves a family. I'll be flying out in a few hours, but with your permission, I would like to be able to call you sometimes to see how Jeremy is doing."

"That's fine. Thanks again." Destiny reached out to embrace Renée.

    Tiffany, Carla, and Marsha stayed with Renée the night before the wedding. They assisted Renée in packing her suitcase for the honeymoon. They took turns telling stories about all of their childhoods. Renée shared the story of how her and Tiffany met. They played a couple of games and then watched a few movies before going to bed. It was a night full of laughter and a lot of fun.

    Renée awaken the next morning to the nice aroma of homemade biscuits, sausage, bacon, grits, and eggs simmering through the house. "Good morning Marsha." Renée said as she walked into the kitchen. "You didn't have to get up and cook anything."

"I know I didn't but I had to make sure you girls had a good breakfast before beginning our busy day. Those babies need at least one good meal before this evening."

Renée kissed her on the cheek. "You are so sweet. Thanks for everything."

"No, thank you for making my baby Ja'Ron the proudest man around. You have brought so much joy to our lives." She smiled.

Tiffany and Carla walked into the kitchen. "Good morning Marsha and Renée."

"Morning," they sang out together.

"Well today is the big day. How do you feel?" Carla asked.

She was blushing like a teenager. "I'm happy to know that in a few hours I'll be Mrs. Ja'Ron Moss." Carla gave her a big hug.

"Okay ladies, breakfast is now ready." They all sat down and enjoyed the food, which was prepared for them. They laughed and talked throughout. After eating, they all begin taking their showers and begun to prepare for the rest of the day.

Tiffany was in the room with Renée completing her make-up when Carla yelled that the limousine had arrived. "Ok we're on our way down," Tiffany yelled back as she placed Renée's veil on her. "You're so beautiful and I'm so happy that you have opened your heart up to love again."

"If it wasn't for you and Keith, none of this would be happening. I'm forever indebted to you both. I love you guys!"

"Oh no, don't start all that mushy stuff. You'll start crying and ruin your make-up and I'm not about to start all over again."

"Whatever Tiff." They both hugged before going downstairs to join Carla and Marsha.

"Where's your gown, Renée?" Carla asked.

"Patti will be bringing it with her. Come on, I don't want to be late for my wedding."

Renée's staff had created a masterpiece of winter wonderland scenery for the ceremony. The lighting was cobalt blue and the room was filled with white birch trees. The chandeliers blended in beautifully with the trees. A snowfall consisted of placing thousands of dainty fresh white flowers on all the tree branches and the room was carpeted in pure white. The chairs were resembled the design of Queen Anne with white upholstery. The programs sat in each chair.

Jeremy, Ja'Ron, and Keith all wore white tuxedos with blue and silver accessories. Patti designed two blue gowns with silver specks throughout for Tiffany and Carla. They looked absolutely gorgeous as they walked down the aisle.

Renée stepped into the entranceway and you could hear the awe's coming from the guest. Patti had designed a beautiful silver wedding gown loaded with pearls and sparkling iridescent stones. She stood there for a few moments sparkling like flawless diamonds. Then she proceeded down the aisle.

"It doesn't make any sense to look that damn good," Regina said to Nia. She continued, "That gown must have cost at least…"

"Shhh..." Nia said. "We'll discuss that later. I don't want to miss a beat tonight."

The reception was just as beautiful. Scenes of a winter forest in silver ink were screened onto tent walls. Different photos of Ja'Ron and Renée were digitally printed on translucent fabric and inserted into the forest. Shimmering silver overlays were thrown over raw silk under lays on the tables. Silver berries graced crisp white napkins neatly folded over elegant silver-edged chargers. Frosted pillar candles in old-fashioned glass lanterns and frosted votives were placed on the tables with white candles lit in them. Majestic Hall was full with over 500 attendants. There were four candelabras on each side of the aisle where the Bridal Party would enter. There were also four birdcages with white doves on each side of the room along the aisle way. Jessica began to introduce the Bridal Party. Once the attendants were seated then the bride and groom were introduced. After they had reached the center of the aisle, they paused, waved, and blew kisses at their guest. As they did this all four cages were unlatched and the doves were released. There were camera flashes going off everywhere. It was absolutely beautiful.

"Renée... girl, this wedding was off the hook! This was totally awesome." Nia and Regina said together.

"Well thank you ladies."

"That gown is... I don't even have the words that would give it justice right now. I'm so overwhelmed with everything. Did Patti make that also?"

"She most certainly did. She's the best."

"You can say that again," said Nia. "We've got to go over and talk to her tonight. Congratulations and we both wish you lots and lots of blessings to come."

"Thank you." They both kissed each side of Renée's cheeks.

Immediately after dinner the cake was cut, they had their first dance as husband and wife. Shortly afterward they had the bouquet toss, in which Carla happened to catch. And the handsome Samuel Hall caught the garter. He's an attorney working at Keith's firm and he had been watching Carla every chance he'd gotten. The night was full of fun and it was a night that would not be forgotten by those in attendance.

    The following morning they left for Hawaii.
"Aloha, my beautiful wife, I love you."
"Aloha, my handsome husband, I love you."
They were there for two weeks. The first week they were alone. The following week Tiffany, Keith, Carla, Marsha, and Jeremy joined them.

SEVEN MONTHS LATER

The doctor looked over the covering draped over her patient. "Renée, this is very important. I know you're ready for this to be over but do not push anymore until I instruct you to do so," the doctor said.

Renée sighed. She was exhausted. Ja'Ron had massaged her back before she decided to lie back. "Is something wrong?" she questioned in a faint tone. She closed her eyes and silently prayed that the baby was fine.

"Everything is under control," the doctor assured her.

Ja'Ron watched the doctor as she continued to work on Renée. Ja'Ron too was a little worried that something was wrong, but he didn't want to alarm his wife. He had to keep her calm. "You're doing great sweetie. I love you so much." He brushed her damp hair back with his hand.

The doctor looked up and nodded at Ja'Ron. "Okay. Here we go Renée, are you ready? Just one more push should do it."

Renée muttered and shook her head. "Ja'Ron I can't. I have no energy left. I can't do it."

"Yes, you can sweetheart. Come on baby, it's almost over. You can do this." He kissed her damp forehead and held her against his strong chest.

The doctor insisted, "Renée you need to push now."

"Come on Renée, take a deep breath and bring our baby into the world."

She took a deep breath. "Ooohhh…" she grunted.

Ja'Ron smiled as he watched the baby slide into the doctor's hand. He was relieved that it was over. Renée had a long labor. "That's it sweetheart. It's all over." He wiped her damp face. "Everything's fine."

"It's a baby girl," the doctor announced. "And she has a good set of lungs too."

Renée gasped as she momentarily closed her eyes, thankful that the delivery was over. The nurse handed the beautiful golden brown cutie to the proud and blushing father. With moist and glistening eyes he held his new baby girl. "Welcome precious, your mommy and daddy loves you. We have been waiting patiently for your arrival. Are you ready to meet your beautiful mother?" He placed her in Renée's arms. She unwrapped her to make sure she had all her fingers and toes. The baby opened her beautiful brown eyes and Renée was filled with joy. She smiled as the tears flowed down her face. "She's perfect."

"What did you expect? We are her parents." Renée smirked as he placed a tender kiss on her lips. "I am the happiest man on earth. I have a beautiful family. Speaking of family, I better go make some phone calls to notify everyone of the baby's arrival."

"Okay. I love you Ja'Ron."

"I love you too sweetheart."

"So what's her name?" Tiffany asked as she brushed the baby's hair. "Her hair is so thick and long."

Renée looked over at her daughter. "Mikaiya Janae Moss. We both have beautiful daughters, Tiffany. What more can we ask for?" She smiled. "Oh, I forgot who I was talking to. Don't feel obligated to answer that Tiffany." They both laughed. "Thanks for everything, Tiffany."

"No, thank you. We've been through a lot together."

"You got that right." Renée replied.

"There's only one thing that I hope for."

"What's that Tiffany?"

"I hope our little girls will carry on our business."

"I'm sure we won't have to worry about that. I can't wait until they are old enough for us to begin teaching them."

The rest of the family walked into the room. "Teaching them what?" Ja'Ron asked. "You two are not already planning for the girls to take over the business, are you?"

Keith quickly blurted out, "I bet they are. You know how they are."

Marsha grinned. "Lord knows we have a family filled with creativity and the knowledge of fashion." They all laughed.

Renée looked around. "Where's Jeremy?"

He came in with flowers for Renée. "Here I am mom." He gave Renée a big kiss on her cheek.

"Thank you sweetie."

"Can I hold her?" Tiffany handed the baby to Ja'Ron.

"Thank you for the flowers Jeremy."

"No problem, mom." Tiffany took him into the restroom to wash his hands.

"Sit over here squirt and I'll help you." Ja'Ron instructed.

Jeremy plopped down in the chair. "Hello Mikaiya. I'm Jeremy, your big, strong brother. I'll teach you a lot of cool stuff; just remember I'm the boss though." He kissed her cheek. "She's pretty. Mom and dad, this is cool. Now I have two people who will look up to me. My sister Mikaiya, and Aunt Tiffany and Uncle Keith's baby Keanna. Aunt Carla, I guess it's your turn to get married next so you can have a baby." Laughter broke out in the room.

"Ha, ha, ha, very funny. Who put him up to saying that?" Everyone shrugged their shoulders announcing, "Not me!"

"Well for all of y'all's information, at this time I'm perfectly happy with my personal life. I don't need and don't want to meet anyone to complicate things for me."

Renée and Tiffany looked at each other. They were thinking the same thing. Those were Renée's same words before she met Ja'Ron. They smiled as both of their eyebrows raised.

"Well Carla, I think you're in trouble now," Keith and Ja'Ron said watching their wives expression.

Renée and Tiffany both shouted in unity, "Aloha!"

Made in the USA